THE ADVENTURES OF THE PANCAKE KNIGHT

Book I Episode I "The Enchiridion"

KaiEl

ISBN: 978-1-953487-03-2 (print)
978-1-953487-04-9 (ebook)

Cover design and all illusrations by the author.

1st Edition printed in USA June, 2023 by Three Knolls Publishing and Printing, Tucson, AZ.

Dedicated.
For those who desire to become the best version of themselves.
Who take the terrifying steps outside of safety and comfort.
Driven by the need to cast out the wretched, wicked temptations of
false gratification through idle distractions.
Who accept their weaknesses, demanding to ignite
the strength within the soul.
Who navigate a society that yearns to consume us and
distract us from our discipline and consistency.
Who dream endlessly.
Who work tirelessly.
Who would choose bone chilling freedom over
foolishly living on our knees.
Who may not have known love, to love with all our hearts.
Who have wronged and been wronged, find the compassion to forgive,
not just others, but themselves.
Who are afraid and alone: bravely walk headlong with
trembling knees and become firestorms in the night.
Who crave honesty, lead by example.
Who build their character when no one is looking.
Who ask not for less problems, but for broader shoulders.
Who seek challenge to foster growth.
Who will restore what is cherished, by restoring ourselves.
Who walk our own path, never walk alone.
Who are not sorry but become better.
Who are self-accountable.
To us.

Day by day, what you choose, what you think and what you do is who
you become. -Heraclitus

Contents

PROLOGUE

The Rabbit and the Wolves

The Eagle Nebula. Located seven-thousand lightyears from Earth. Within its vast, vivid clouds of stellar gases and dust, the Pillars of Creation usher in newborn stars. Surrounded by primeval celestial bodies shimmering in the backdrop of the universe as neighboring solar systems orbit around themselves in their endless ballet. From a distant vantagepoint, the chaos of the universe is shrouded in an illusion of tranquility through the deafening silence.

But in a fraction of a second, that veil of tranquility was shattered as an onslaught of cannons, explosions, and screeching starships cut through the quiet delusion. From the now-theater of war, a single cruiser attempts to evade destruction from three pursuing vessels. Wounded and unable to return fire, the lone ship's sole course of action is to remain in one piece.

The floundering ship approached a massive spatial anomaly. Dust clouds churned with violence and dark energy as lightning ripped through the raging gale. In a dire attempt to shake off its attackers, the cruiser plunged headfirst into the squall's maw, followed by its assailants.

Dodging projectiles, dropping chaff flares, and squeezing through colliding space rocks, the ship refused to succumb to its fate. As the skirmish entered a clearing in the storm, the cruiser was left vulnerable away from the cover of asteroids. The attackers locked on the vessel and fired, critically striking their prey, and pulled out of the storm.

The ship sputtered as onboard systems failed one after the other. Not before a small pod jettisoned from the mangled cruiser and out of the space storm. The ship, unwilling to go quietly into the night, ignited its engines into full power. In a final battle cry, the cruiser lurched forward before the engines blew, and all systems shut down.

The perished cruiser plummeted through the maelstrom before being caught by an unknown pull of gravity. The gale revealed a static image of an enormous blue world, streaked with wisps of white clouds and green land hidden behind a cloak that could not have been seen without the storm's interference. The vessel burst into flames as it pierced the atmosphere and tumbled into the terrestrial world.

From the surface of the planet, the destruction of the ship appeared as nothing more than a bright shooting star. Under tremendous pressure, the vessel was ripped into five fragments that scattered across the planet. The remains that did not burn up in reentry were trailed by fire and pluming smoke as they shrieked through the air. With a thunderous crash, the debris collided into terra firma.

CHAPTER I

I Remember You in the Lifestream

ONE YEAR LATER

The blue green marbled planet, Keevah, entered the electromagnetic wave of nebulous gases as it did every year. From the surface, the space current interacting with the magnetosphere displayed a multitude of auroras, brilliant shooting stars, and ethereal booms that accompanied the cosmic lightning storm in the sky above. To the inhabitants of this planet, it was an indicator of the changing seasons, and for many, the arrival of the holiday season.

Though Keevahlings understood what the storm was, they were at a loss as to its origins. They called it, the Lifestream. However, the creation mythos of the annual phenomena had been passed down in tales of magical lore, ancient gods, and fabled history. Although it had been shrouded in stories and different faiths, one thing everyone agreed on was its name, bestowed upon it in a long-forgotten language, Coi Kelume. This tongue was so old, its genesis was anyone's guess. But the celebrations during this holiday centered around one thing: life.

Today, with the ever-accelerating growth of modern advancements and product consumption, the foundational ingredients of valuing life, honoring self-worth, the natural world, and the importance of one another had turned this celestial event into nothing more than a time to exchange gifts. In the mountain-forest town of Lemnear, the Lifestream was nothing out of the ordinary beyond an annual holiday. It was like any other sunrise, sunset, or phases of the planets and moons. It was considered mundane to all but one:

A pint-sized fluffy brown walrus with a face full of whiskers and two curved tusks named Bort.

Bort's curiosity and imagination more than made up for his walnut-sized brain. Standing on the observation deck of his treehouse he'd aptly dubbed Castle Bort, situated high above his home among the canopy of the giant sequoias Lemnear is known for, Bort adjusted the lens on his well-worn telescope. It wasn't uncommon to spot Bort dreaming high into the heavens on any given day, but in the late evening sky, painted in permanent twilight, with the Lifestream highlighting the distant nebulas and celestial bodies made gazing into the sky this night extra special.

Bort turned his attention from his telescope and made sure he had everything he needed for the night. Favorite snacks and drinks? Check. Toys, books, and games to help pass the excruciating wait? Check. Nest of blankets and pillows? Check! Pleased, Bort smiled, thrilled he would be sleeping under the neon sky tonight, and returned to his telescope. Bort had known the tales about the Lifestream and what it represented for as long as he had been in Lemnear. But now, after so long, he felt excited to see it for the first time without extrapolating the Lifestream from his surreal and broken memory.

Bort had no recollection of observing the Lifestream nor the legends woven from it as he searched through his shattered memories. The earliest memories, or as he called them, "remembories," were of what his friends had told him. Last year during the Lifestream, Bort was found wandering the Lemnear forest, dazed, confused, and with a grapefruit-sized bump on his head. He would learn later that he suffered from severe amnesia, likely caused by the unknown trauma to his head. Thinking about the injury made Bort rub the old site of the lump. All that remained now was his soft, fuzzy noggin. But touching the right spot made Bort wince in pain as paralyzing electricity shot through his body and blanked out his thoughts.

The pain was a harsh reminder that amnesia still plagued him. Healers called the symptom phantom pain, and it cursed him even now. Bort pulled his eye from the lens of the telescope and rubbed around the old injury. Frustrating as it was, there was only so much he could do about it. But he couldn't help the flurry of muddled thoughts and emotions his amnesia provoked, leaving only bread-crumbs to grasp at. Bort's thoughts billowed in sync with the Lifestream in the evening sky.

Who was Bort, where did he come from, and why was he so fond of stinky cheese? All these questions remained without answer. No matter how hard he tried to remember, it was always pushed back into the vault of his mind by the phantom pain. And, with any answer Bort dug up, ten more questions sprouted from it, and then ten more.

Bort brought his flipper down from his head and stared at it. Rubbing his flippers together, he felt his warm and fuzzy skin that blanketed him. Bort was soft and squishy, while others were of bone and sinew. Although Bort was just like everyone else, someone who ate, slept, pooped, burped, and snored, he knew he was different. In all Lemnear, there was no one that came close to being his kin. The closest likeness to Bort were the plush toys he saw at the Lemnear market.

Bort glanced up from his flippers and became aware of his body. In his chest, Bort's heart surged with love and kindness. His brain brimmed with imagination inside his skull. His guts hungered for never-ending adventure and pancakes in his belly. His lungs filled with laughter, and his eyes glazed over with the dreams and excitement of life. Bort lowered his head and rubbed his flippers together once more. Even though the toys appeared to be his nearest relatives, they were lifeless and dull.

Questions like these popped into Bort's mind often, even to this day. No matter how hard he grappled with his amnesia, Bort couldn't remember anything beyond a year ago. Bort could only speculate about himself and of things he did not understand. But Bort being Bort, he found his own unique answers that satisfied him for the time being. Who was Bort? Well, Bort was Bort! Where did he come from? Where his feet brought him, of course. Why was he so fond of stinky cheese?

Bort chewed his lip and furrowed his brow. Well, maybe some things are best left to being a mystery, he thought, scratching his chin. With that, Bort nodded, smiled, and shrugged. Finding his newfound perspectives on his churning questions gave way to his cheerful disposition. His answers satisfied him well enough, at least for now. Bort looked back up into the night sky. Here, high up on Castle Bort was where he could empty his tangled thoughts, feel the clearest in his mind, and renew his determination to unravel the amnesia that shrouded his past.

"Bort," a feminine voice sung out to him.

Bort turned his attention to see Garlic, a fiery red-haired woman, surfing up through the canopy on her staff named Ashgrowl. Ashgrowl sounded like a blowtorch as Garlic flew in a corkscrew path trailed by flows of magic. Her long locks cascaded around her as she jumped off the staff and onto the castle's deck. Her ears were long with a small nose distinct with hundreds of freckles, telltale traits of gnomes. Her light skin accentuated the depth of blues from her large almond eyes. Dressed in tight leggings with a pack on her side, a belt slotted with potions, a buttoned sleeveless blouse, and a flower for a cap, she landed with the grace and muteness of a feline, stopping her momentum by placing her gloved palm on the floor while her long hair cascaded around her. Getting to her feet, she dusted off.

Bort smiled and waved to her as she approached. "Bo(Garlic!)rt!" he said in a melodic tone.

Bort! Was all Garlic or anyone else ever heard him say when he spoke. She smiled, remembering the time when it sounded like nothing more than gibberish to her. Now, Garlic was well acquainted with his peculiar way of speaking and understood him with crystalline clarity. To the untrained ear, Bort's language was as nonsensical as his dancing. His borts were constructed with a variety of inflections, animated facial expressions, and dramatic body language. Garlic shook her head, it was effortless to understand him, if she took the time to listen.

Garlic closed her eyes, flipped her hair, and ran a hand through its length before she opened her eyes. Her gaze locked with Bort's as her smile grew, and she dashed towards him. "Bort!" Garlic exclaimed with her arms outstretched.

Bort braced himself with open arms. There was a price to pay for being so soft and squishy, but one he didn't mind paying in the least. In one fell swoop, Garlic snatched him up for a tight hug, squeezing him to her as Bort wrapped his flippers as best he could around her. "It's so good to see you, Bort! Thanks for inviting me to watch the Lifestream with you," she said.

"Bo(I couldn't imagine seeing it without my good friends!)rt!" he said, expressing his sincerity with a tighter hug.

Garlic smiled and squeezed him tighter one last time before putting him down where he looked up at Garlic. Even though Garlic was a gnome, she held quite the height advantage over him. If he stood tall with good posture, the crown of his head made it up to the bottom of her chest line. Bort smiled and waddled back to the telescope, adjusting it once more as Garlic grabbed some snacks and drinks from the pile and took a seat in the nest of pillows and blankets. Satisfied with his adjustments of the telescope, Bort plopped down next to Garlic, where they both stared to the heavens in silence.

"Hmm…" Garlic chuckled. "I can't believe it has been about a year since I found you. It all has gone by in the blink of an eye," Garlic said, breaking the silence.

"Bo(Whoa! Has it been? It sure hasn't felt that long at all. I feel like I got here only yesterday.)rt," he said.

Garlic tucked her knees to her chest and hugged them close, with her eyes trained on the night sky. "Oh Bort, the more I think of it, back then was like a carnival every day. Wasn't it so nice? Crazy circus we thought would last forever. I remembered when I first met you…" Garlic said. She turned her gaze to Bort, laying her cheek on her knees. "Do you remember that day?" she asked, cautious and attentive to his response.

Bort turned away from her and looked to the sky. He put a flipper to his chin and then played with his tusks, deep in thought. Bort sat straight up in a blur, throwing his arms into the air with a gasp. "Bo(I remember! I remember!)rt!" he said, delighted. "Bo(It all started one day…)rt…" Bort began.

CHAPTER II

Stranger in a Strange Land

ONE YEAR EARLIER…

Bort held a large lump on his head that throbbed with every step he took as he emerged from the shadows of a deep woodland. Disoriented and tripping over his own feet, he blinked nonstop, trying to clear his hazy vision. Pain shot through his body like electricity as Bort's constitution adapted to the pain. He took ample moments before he tolerated the sting, regained his sight, and beheld his surroundings.

The ground beneath Bort's feet felt soft, moist, and squishy. Cradling his head, Bort looked to his feet and marched in place. The mushy sounds his steps made was amusing, and it helped distract him from his injury. Bort looked up and found himself standing in an old-growth forest covered with ancient green vegetation and a thick layer of moss. The giant sequoia trees that inhabited these woods stood strong, and scraped the heavens above.

Bort oohed at the colossal trees, struggling to keep from falling over as he tried to catch a glimpse of the canopies. Iridescent colors from glowing flora accented the deep hues of the lush green woods. Bort brought his flipper to his side and looked around. The forest was so bright and full of life that it made it hard to believe it was nighttime. It was like nothing he had ever seen before! Bort began plodding along, his head on a swivel, noticing every neat sight along his undetermined path.

A distant muffled boom echoed throughout the forest. Grabbing Bort's attention, he looked behind him in the direction of where the sound seemed to originate. Seeing only shadows within the beautiful shimmering woods, Bort turned back onto his path and moved into a tall grass clearing. Wondering what that sound could have been, he looked down at his flippers. Could it have been

thunder? He thought, but he didn't feel any raindrops. Bort scrunched his face, contemplating the noise and continued walking, not noticing a sleeping school of manta rays. Spooking each other, Bort jumped back, and the school took flight up into the canopy where Bort, amazed at their beauty, followed them with his gaze.

Bort's eyes widened, and his heart skipped a beat. "Bor—" was all he could say as his eyes filled with the sight of the cloudless night sky through the trees. The Lifestream was in full swing, and the colors swirled into one another, littered with shooting stars, as the school of manta rays sailed out of sight. Yet, something else hung in the lower atmosphere. It was strange and out of place in the sky that night. A streak of black, wispy smoke cut through the air.

Bort tracked the trail that led behind him. Whatever that smoke was from punched holes through the canopy. A sickening plume of smoke billowed up not far from where he'd emerged. It boggled his brain to guess what it could be. But the more he thought about it, the more Bort's head throbbed. He grimaced, put a flipper to his head, and any remaining thoughts he had, scattered.

Bort shook the pain away, and his spellbound eyes locked back onto the incredible sky. He stared into the cosmos with dilated pupils with the stars reflecting in his gaze. Bort sat down and held onto his feet, admiring the changing colors and billowing space clouds. Bort's head felt foggy, and it was hard to retain any memory. He wasn't sure if he was awake or dreaming. Among the tranquil noises of the forest came a twinkling sound that caught Bort's attention. Tiny silver sparkling motes of dust floated down to the ground from a white porcelain moon-butterfly that was wisped with florescent blue patterns. It fluttered in front of Bort and rested on a single blade of stargrass.

Enthralled, Bort crawled on his belly to get a closer look. He was able to see its fuzzy antennae before the moon-butterfly took flight once again. Bort followed it for a while, watching it land on different rocks and plants, traversing his way through the forest. The moon-butterfly flew over a stream, into the air, and up through the trees. Bort hopped as high as he could to try and take off with it. But alas, he remained earthbound. Bort smiled, waved fair-winds, and then returned his attention to the forest.

Bort found himself at the edge of a road. Across the way, a sign next to a wooden shack contained a bench. It was a simple structure made of oak, but ornate with designs and colors that matched the look and feel of the forest. Ambient lighting came from tiny glowing plants on the floor and a paper lantern hung in the middle of the structure with a swirled design that resembled a shell. Bort studied the area with a flipper pressed to his mouth. What is this weird place? The sign had a snail on it. Looks delicious, but what does it mean?

Not having to wait long to find out, Bort heard an indistinguishable rumbling in the distance. It sounded like a combination of slithering and boulders rolling downhill. Soon after, a slimy head with two protruding eyeballs on long stalks poked up from the hillside, followed by an ornate shell in a distinct green color climbed over the horizon. It was a snail! But not just any snail, it was a huge one!

Bort licked his chops and began to drool, rubbing his flippers together. He had not eaten for, well — he couldn't remember. But he did know his appetite was intense, and it was his favorite dish coming to meet him. Bort's eyes glinted with hunger as the giant snail stopped right beside him.

The snail, unaware he was on the dinner menu tonight, waited for Bort to embark with eyes half closed and locked forward on the road ahead. Not feeling Bort climb aboard, the snail snuck a quick glance at his tiny rider. The snail's eyes widened, surprised to see his teeny passenger latched to the side of his tail, flailing. The snail took a closer look to see what the walrus was doing. He'd never seen such behavior from a rider before. The snail thought maybe he was due to be cleaned. But he wasn't at the station yet. He felt very confused.

Bort tried to take a chomp out of the snail and wriggled like a fish on a hook, struggling to sink his bite. But the snail's hide was so slimy and tough, Bort could not even drill a tusk in. Besides, it tasted like hot, salty garbage. Bort detached his maw from the snail, leaving a vague imprint of his mouth along with dribbles of saliva. His tongue flopped out, and he wiped it with his flippers. Spluttering and spitting, Bort turned around to jump off his would-be prey only to encounter a giant eyeball.

"Bort!" Bort squealed in a panic and threw his flippers into the air. The eyeball alone was five times his size! Puzzled, the snail examined Bort, never seeing anything like this before. Nervous sweat appeared on Bort's forehead as he put his flippers behind his head and laughed. His little mind worked as fast as it could to make up an excuse. But lying wasn't one of Bort's strongest talents.

Figuring this funny little walrus didn't know about the snail-bus service, and having a schedule to keep, the snail stretched out his long neck and grabbed Bort with his mouth to place him atop his shell. For Bort, the enormous gaping jaws from the snail signaled that the dinner menu had just switched places. Bort shot into a floundering panic as the snail's head loomed over him and his mouth began to open. Bort thought he was about to become snail chow! He bumbled down the snail's tail and was about to skedaddle into the safety of the woods. But

before Bort could run away screaming into the forest, the snail caught a gentle clasp on the nape of Bort's neck. Bort yelped, feeling the snail grab hold of him, and he clung onto patches of grass for dear life. But without much struggle, the grassroots gave way, and Bort went sailing through the air, gripping a chunk of sod in each flipper.

The giant eyes of the snail examined Bort as he screamed and thrashed around. Flailing for so long, Bort grew tired and accepted defeat. Whatever the snail was going to do with him sure was taking a long time. Bort went slack, hung like fresh laundry on a clothesline, and rotated in the snail's mouth with a frustrated look on his face. However, once the snail felt Bort relax, he placed him delicately atop its shell. Once aboard, Bort sighed in relief; he wasn't going to become a tasty snack. Right then, his whole demeanor changed with a renewed love for life.

"Bo(Wowie!)rt!" Bort said as he looked around, still holding onto the chunks of grass. The shell was outfitted with benches, railings, posters, vid screens, and digital displays that ran across the railings showing a strange language adorning the top of the snail's shell. The add-ons imitated the snail's shell and looked almost as if they were indeed part of the snail. The deck beneath his feet was shiny and spiraled, just like the pattern of the snail with the same beautiful hues of green.

A bell chimed, and the red lights of the railing display switched to yellow and then to green. Once the final bell sounded, Bort felt the ground beneath him lurch as the snail moved forward, causing him to stumble. Bort caught himself before falling over, which pulled him back from admiring the workmanship of the bus. Bort reached up on his tippy toes to one of the dangling handles from the bars and steadied himself.

Moments later, Bort bounced with great enthusiasm, gripping the handrail, enjoying the ride. Next to him sat an elderly possum-lady with her nose buried in a book. Bort smiled a tusky grin and waived hello to the woman. She didn't notice him, so Bort stood high on his tippy toes, extended his neck, and waved with greater purpose. The old lady blinked her eyes, with one eyelid lagging just behind the other, ran her thumb down her tongue and turned the page of her book. His hello ignored and his arm going numb, Bort decided to keep to himself and savor the new experience.

With another ring of the bell, a blue light flashed, as did an animated screen that showed a person standing and another sitting, both of which were strapped into some sort of contraption. Bort, confused, looked at the possum-lady to see what she would do. Unaffected by the warning, the elderly lady continued with her book. Seeing her do nothing, Bort shrugged and did the same, mirroring the lady's same dead-eyed expression.

The snail approached a tree, which it ascended without a hitch. In an instant, the bus went vertical, and gravity transferred from below Bort's feet.

"Bo(W-woah!)rt!" Bort exclaimed, losing his footing. He felt that sinking, falling feeling before skidding down the surface. Bort reacted without thought and caught on one of the rails that flew past him with a clank. Horrified, he stared at his glossy reflection in the floor, which was now a wall in front of him. Staring into his green tinted reflection, it all clicked together in his brain. The bells, lights, and pictures that displayed a moment earlier all made sense. He looked over to the old possum-lady, who now hung on by her tail. Unaffected by the shift in perspective, she once again licked her finger and turned the page of her book. Bort struggled with all his might and pulled himself into one of the straps. Once he was able to tie himself in, Bort held onto the fastenings for dear life, shaking like a pressure cooker. After a few minutes, the snail-bus became horizontal, and a bell chimed, giving the go-ahead to unfasten seatbelts. However, Bort stayed clinched onto his fastenings, untrusting of the all-clear signal, terrified it would happen again.

Arriving at her stop, the old possum closed her book, rose to her feet with the aid of a cane, and shuffled past the tiny walrus, who clung onto the harness with a death grip, trembling in fear, and a clump of grass clenched in each flipper. Bort tracked her with his eyes as she ambled by him, oblivious to Bort, and disembarked. It wasn't much longer after that the now-familiar ding of the bus chimed, and the snail-bus embarked towards its final stop for the night.

Minutes later, the bus arrived at the last bus station, where the bell sounded. "Thank you for riding the Slug-Lug Express. Final stop, Watertail Plaza," a voice spoke through the intercom. The bus dinged, turned off its lights, and slithered away to retire for the evening, leaving its last, lone passenger standing at the bus station with a blank and happy expression coating his face. Bort looked around and dropped the clods of grass from his flippers. This bus station was constructed using the giant mushroom pads that scattered the nearby forest!

Raising his foot into the air, Bort stepped down on one of the mushroom pads, which sprung like a trampoline. Surprised, Bort kept his eyes on his feet and stomped hard, sending him a few inches in the air. Bort stood motionless while his bouncing faded into stillness. Bort's pupils dilated. Unable to contain his excitement, he jumped up and thumped on the mushroom, sending himself high into the air and releasing spores that filled the night like a gentle swarm of moths.

Bort once again stood still, and he watched the spores float into the air. The spores glowed in different arrays of pale light the moment they caught the currents of the wind, and they circled Bort like fallen petals in spring. Bort shut his eyes, brought his flippers to his face and shook with exhilaration.

Bort gave in to temptation and threw himself at the mushrooms. He bounded and flapped his flippers in the air, trying with each jump to flip higher through the crisp night. In his enthusiasm, Bort soon lost control of his jumps and slipped off the pad, landing on the forest floor headfirst with a loud bonk. Bort sat himself up and held his head as his eyes swirled in their sockets.

Bort sat against the stem of the mushroom, allowing the nausea and throbbing pain to pass. Sitting there, recovering, he observed his surroundings. He was now in a town with many different buildings. Several lined the forest floor, others spiraled up around the giant tree trunks, and some were nestled within hillsides and roots. The structures matched the same forest colors of the woods, just like the little hut at the roadside. Each structure had colorful glowing signs and ornate art, along with beautiful carvings and busts that extended into the pathways. The design of the town was planned out with careful intention, and the transition between forest and village was seamless.

Bort's curiosity overrode his pain and got him to his feet to continue exploring. Bort walked with one flipper on his tusk and the other on his head down the cobblestone pathways, admiring the many sculptures and designs beneath his feet depicting different elements and symbols.

One of the stone inlays in the roadway caught Bort's attention. It was a depiction of mushrooms, not unlike the bouncy mushrooms from before. Bort Looked behind him and could no longer see the mushroom bus station. Somewhat disappointed, he wasn't sure if he could find his way back to play on them again. He scowled, forgetting why he'd stopped jumping on them in the first place. Bort did his best to look up at his forehead for the answer but only found pulsating pain.

With a huff, Bort gave up thinking, since the thumping ache intensified the more he pondered the question. His gaze went back down to the mushroom inlay. Just in front of that one laid another tile, then another, and another! Bort followed them until there were no more. Standing in front of the last mushroom inlay, he looked up. His flippers dropped from his tusk and head as his jaw dropped to the floor. In front of Bort, giant mushrooms grew all around him and up the giant sequoias.

This is where the extra-bouncy mushrooms must be. But he had to make sure. "Bo(I'm a try science!)rt!" he shouted with his flippers in the air and sprinted towards the toadstools. Midway, Bort bounded towards the mushrooms, rolled into a ball, and launched himself at them. Bort was shot into the air twice as high as the mushrooms by the station. These were even better than he'd expected. These were jam-packed with spores that glittered around him like falling snow. Best of all, they made bouncy sounds when he leapt off them.

CHAPTER III

I Won't Forget the World We Lost

Hmm, hmm, hmm…" Garlic sung to herself as she collected a few medicinal mushrooms and herbs. As the apothecary to Lemnear, Garlic made potions, tinctures, liniments, ointments, medicines, and poultices to help heal the sick and injured. The mushroom farmer, Myco, grew medicinal mushrooms along the pathways in town to be picked by the villagers if they fell ill. However, the rarer ones he grew for Garlic were nearby his home. In thanks, Garlic would leave a basket of balms and potions for the old farmer to help with his health and keep him spry in his older age.

A cloud of spores drifted over to Garlic and distracted her from her foraging. Confused, she looked in the direction of Myco's house. "Huh? I thought the old man was out foraging mushrooms for a few weeks. Did he get back? Why is he releasing spores at such an odd hour?" Garlic said aloud, studying the spores in the air. She got to her feet and dusted herself off, collecting her things before making her way over to Myco's house to investigate.

An odd rhythmic pinging echoed down the path as she turned the corner to Myco's house. Among the giant mushrooms, she saw a little brown walrus ping-ponging between the pads. Sometimes he would jump, other times, he would flip, but favored holding onto his feet and allowed the mushrooms to bounce him around like a ball in a pinball machine.

Garlic froze, surprised to see some outsider bouncing among the mushrooms. "Who is that?" she said to herself as she ran towards the stranger. Once in earshot, she shouted with authority to the little walrus, "Hey!"

Airborne and upside down, Bort turned his attention to a weird-looking girl frowning up at him with fists on her hips. He gave a pleasant wave with a musical "Bort" as a greeting.

"What are you doing? Myco's gonna be furious! You're gonna be in big trouble, mister!" Garlic shouted.

Bort cocked his head. "Bo(Myco what's a Myc—?)r—?" he said. But before Bort could finish his sentence, he hit the rim of one of the mushrooms. This had so much spring, it sounded like a ricochet and sent Bort flying off in an arched trajectory, twinkling off into the horizon. Bort's thrilled shriek faded off into silence as he rocketed into the distance. "Bo(Bye-bye nice lady...)rt..." he said with haste before his voice faded off into the distance.

Garlic reared her head back, confused. "Wha—? 'bort'? What's bort mean?" she said. As Bort blasted off, it caught her by surprise. "Huh? Hey! Come back here!" she demanded, following hot on his trail.

Garlic's footfalls echoed off the cobblestone path, her heart pounding in her ears. Approaching the stream that ran through town brought her to a halt. She used this moment to catch her breath. Losing track of the walrus somewhere between the market and the secret hollow grove district, Garlic looked in all directions hoping to spot any trace of him. "Huff... where... puff... did he go? Huff..." she said in between breaths.

From high in the distance, an excited squeal broke through the silence, first as a whisper and then grew louder.

"Boooorrrrrrt!" the little walrus yelled as he made splashdown in the river in front of Garlic. Garlic brought her hands up, and made a futile attempt to protect herself from the torrent of water that soaked her thoroughly. "Ugh!" she gasped in shock, and shook off any water she could. Garlic pulled her flower cap off, wrung it out, and placed the now-squished flower atop her head. Composing herself, Garlic looked up to meet a tiny brown head peering out at her from within the stream. "Y-you!" Garlic said, pointing at him with ire.

Bort stared at her with a blank expression. "Bo(hello!)rt!" he sung out to her with a single playful flipper splashing up from the water, waving at her.

"Get out of there right now, mister!" Garlic demanded, shooting her fists to her sides and stomping her feet.

There was silence for a moment as Garlic stared at Bort with fire in her eyes; while Bort returned her gaze with a whimsical expression.

...Dunk!

Without a word, Bort shot himself underwater, and the water's surface went calm.

"H-hey!" Stunned, Garlic shouted and ran to the edge of the water. Staring into it, she could only see her obscured reflection and the backdrop of the town. Her face contorted in frustration as she plunged her arm deep into the stream, attempting to noodle him out. Groping around, her hand gripped something squishy. "Ha! Gotcha!" she said with a smirk and pulled. Once her arm came out of the water, she was about to give the walrus an earful. However, her face contorted into one of pure horror and disgust; she wasn't looking at a little walrus, but at a giant wriggling starlight slug.

"Eek!" she screamed and held the slug far away from her body. Garlic shut her eyes and turned away as it writhed in her hand. Time seemed to slow as Garlic held the slug away from her body to drop it back in the river before a giant fountain of water rose from the stream. With hearts in his eyes, Bort flung himself from the water, swallowing the slug whole along with Garlic's arm up to her elbow. Shocked, Garlic turned back, wide-eyed, to Bort as he met her gaze with the same blissful blank stare. Once time resumed to normal, the two stared at one another motionless for a second before...

"Yah!" Garlic screamed, violently swinging her arm, trying to shake Bort off.

Bort jostled around, wildly borting, before letting go and kerplunking back into the water as Garlic fell backward.

Garlic sat up and shut her eyes as tight as she could, doing her best to shake the horrendous sight of the slug from her memory. However, when she raised her saliva-coated hand to her head, it only etched it into her mind.

"Ah! Ew! Gross!" she said, standing up with the viscous spit dripping from her limb. Garlic snarled and shook her arm, splattering slobber onto the cobblestone pathway.

"Argh! That's it!" Garlic exclaimed. She held her palms in front of her and braced herself with her legs. "Nid!" she commanded.

Faster than a gunshot, a gust of wind snapped around Garlic, blowing her hair and clothing around. Her shoulders shuttered, absorbing a massive kinetic blast, laying grass sideways and sending pebbles flying. The atmospheric pressure around her cracked through the air as a one-meter distorted sphere impacted the water. The burst sent water raining down all around and exposed the riverbed for a moment before it was swallowed back up by the churning waters. Bort, being just outside the blast, rode the force of the shockwave, which carried him into the air like a ragdoll alongside big waves of water.

Bort was whisked up into the sky and enjoyed the rush of tumbling about in the waters over the town. He was thrilled as he somersaulted back down towards the stream. Right before he plunged back into the water, Garlic lunged forward to catch him. But Bort was too slick, and he slipped out of her grasp, disappearing into the stream. Garlic was giving it her all, but for Bort, it was playtime. Bort shot up from the bottom of the water, held onto his feet, and stuck his tongue out at her. Garlic's eyes flared, filled with fire, and she lunged at him again with the same result.

Bort would jump out of the river, strike a pose, and contort his body just outside of Garlic's grasp. As it soon became a game for him. Not long after, Bort didn't have to propel himself out to the surface, as Garlic's fury bloomed, and she hurled bombardments of kinetic blasts into the waters. However, it only enhanced Bort's amusement, as he could now flip through the air, displaying his acrobatic prowess. Their game went on and on. Bort's deep belly laughter was second only to Garlic's growing fury.

Garlic fell back on the bank of the stream, soaked, out of breath, and depleted of mana. "Huff... F-fine... Puff... Stay in the water for all I care," Garlic said, waving him off and propping herself up with her palms.

Bort gawked at Garlic with a blank and blissful expression, his eyes just above the waterline, and hoped to continue their game. But seeing Garlic breathing hard with her head tossed back, exhausted, he figured the game was over. Bort took his time swimming over to the riverbank and once again, submerged himself. Everything fell silent before Bort splashed up from the brook, plopped himself onto dry land, and slapped his flippers at the edge of the stream.

Bort used his tusks to anchor himself at the bank of the river. Amidst grunts and maximum effort, Bort's muscles trembled as he struggled to pull himself out of the water. Bort's graceful aquatic acrobatics vanished, replaced with blundering endeavors to get his feet onto dry land.

"Bo(Hmph! Whoops! That's okay. I'll get it next try.)rt," Bort said to himself as his foot slipped off the bank and back into the water. "Bo(Okay! Here I go again! This time I'll do it for sure! Hmph! Rats! One more time...)rt..." He continued mumbling motivational words to himself as he worked.

Garlic had caught her breath minutes ago and now watched the walrus struggle to get out of the stream. Seeing the dramatic change in Bort's athleticism left her at a loss for words. Bort's eyes darted to his left, spotting a bush of water pokitails growing nearby. He grabbed onto them, yanked himself out, and plonked belly-down on the earth. He celebrated with victorious borty fanfare and raised his flippers into the air. Exhausted, Bort dropped them to the ground, out of breath. After a quick recovery, Bort rolled onto his back like a hot dog and lumbered to his feet. His soft body sagged, drenched. Bort looked over at Garlic with a delighted smile and wandered over to her, his feet squishing against the cobblestone path. They stared at one another before Garlic stifled a snort and broke into a fit of laughter, which then rubbed off on Bort, who laughed out loud with her.

"Bo(Hello! My name is Bort! Thanks for playing with me, nice lady! I sure had a lotta fun!)rt!" Bort said with his flippers outstretched from his sides, letting the water drip from his body.

Puzzled, Garlic cocked her head. "Bort? Is Bort your name?" she asked.

Bort smiled and wobbled his head up and down.

Garlic stared at him a moment and put a hand to her chest. "My name is

Garlic. Garlic Celhana," she said.

Bort's smile grew broad and nodded his head with more zing; causing his injury to throb. Bort winced in pain and shot his flippers to his head. "Bo(Owie… I think I hurt my head.)rt," he said. Bort's face contorted into anguish while tears formed in his eyes.

Garlic pulled her knees to her body and leaned forward. "Did you bump your head?" she said, beginning to understand him.

Bort grew anxious while observing his surroundings. His gaze wandered off towards the distance, turning his confusion into uneasiness. his face began to gnarl with worry, and his eyes darted around, looking for anything familiar. Taking in the alien scenery, his face filled with a weighty expression of dread. Bort glanced in every direction before focusing down on the ground beneath his feet.

It seemed to Garlic that, for the first time, Bort realized his predicament. With his flippers cradling his head, Bort looked up into Garlic's eyes. "Bo(I… I don't know where I am) rt," he said with pure honesty. "Bo(I think I'm lost!)rt," he added with quaking panic in his voice.

Bort's childlike innocence dismissed any suspicions Garlic had had about him. His demeanor and genuine tone were more than enough to convince her. As the apothecary, she figured the trauma to his head was responsible for his confused actions. "Are you lost? Where did you come from?" she asked as he became easier to understand.

Bort turned his eyes from Garlic as he tried to recall how he got here. He turned around to look at where he'd come, before he sniffled and hiccupped. Bort faced Garlic with snot and tears streaming down his face. "Bo(I-I don't re-member,)rt," he stuttered and began to cry.

Garlic's shoulders relaxed with a lengthy sigh through her nose as a consoling smile sprouted on her face. She sympathized with Bort and, at the same time, began to comprehend his naivety. Bort buried his tear-filled eyes with his flippers. "Bo(I'm — sniff — so — hic — scared!)rt!" he cried out.

Bort stared up at Garlic. Her gaze felt full of genuine care. Alone in this strange place, Garlic felt like a warm glimmer of hope. She did play with him this whole time, after all. It was then when he decided to confide in her and broke down into a full cry. Bort stumbled over to her and spread his flippers, desperate for a hug.

Garlic's heart twinged as she moved to her knees and hugged the sopping-wet walrus, causing water to squish out of him. Bort didn't feel like a regular person. He was spongy like cotton, yet warm and firm as if made of sinew. His skin felt soft, fluffy, and gentle to the touch. Bort spoke with his heart, free of any maliciousness, which dissolved any emotional barriers Garlic held up.

"Hey, hey, now, it's okay… There, there…" Garlic said in a tender tone and hugged him tighter. "Don't worry. You're safe with me. I'll take care of you, okay, Bort?" she added to calm him.

Bort pulled away from Garlic, doing his best to stifle his tears. He nodded slowly, his gaze fixated on the ground, and wiped his face with his flipper. Garlic stood to her feet and took hold of Bort's flipper. He was small compared to her; however, his flippers were enormous! They engulfed her tiny hand. Garlic looked at their clasped hands; his grip was firm yet gentle. Bort turned his attention to Garlic and stared up at her, enamored. Bort wiped the tears and snot from his face and sniffled. "Bo(Thank you so much, Garlic. I'm super glad I met you.)rt," he said. Bort's words showed but a fraction of what his genuine smile said.

Garlic smiled, hoping to get Bort back to being the curious, happy creature she'd met earlier. Garlic bent down and spoke tenderly near his ear. "C'mon, Bort. Let's get you somewhere warm and dry. You're soaked. Let's clean you up, little piggy," she said with a giggle.

Bort waddled next to her, his flipper sticking all but straight up as Garlic held it.

"Bo(I sure liked swimming.)rt," he said in between sobs, still trying to get ahold of himself as they walked down the path towards Garlic's house.

CHAPTER IV

Late But Not Forgotten

PRESENT DAY

Wrappers laid strewn about Castle Bort. Plates of food had slices missing from them, drink canisters laid about empty, and the teapot was lighter. The snacks and drinks Bort had laid out had dwindled to half their glory.

Bort stared off into the sky as he described the tale of their first encounter. Garlic watched Bort the entire time, resting her cheek on her knees and cradling her legs as she recalled the memories with fond emotions. Once he finished, she smiled before turning her attention up into the sky alongside him. The colors in the heavens pulsed and changed from greens to blues to reds, forming many different patterns. Her heart filled with happiness, knowing that although Bort had lost everything, including his memory, from that day on, he was able to remember even the littlest details.

Just before Garlic could comment on the memory, a female voice rang out from below the deck. "Hey! Sorry, I'm late!"

The sound of buzzing wings filled the gap between silence and the omnipotent sounds of the Lifestream. A well-defined, womanly silhouette shot up into the canopy of the trees and flew straight towards them, landing like a ghost at the edge of the deck. Without a studder in her landing, a young Beylan walked towards Bort and Garlic. They saw adorned on her abdomen the signature black

and yellow rings as she stepped into the light. Her long, voluminous, dark green windswept hair was covered in glowing, multicolored pollen; same for the furs on her legs and all four of her arms. She removed the goggles from her large, dark amber almond eyes and moved them up to her hair as a makeshift hairband just in front of her antennae. She flattened her wings to her back and brushed her hand through her long mane, which settled inches from the ground. She wore thigh-high black socks, short-cut jean shorts, and a black Metalskulls band shirt.

"I lost track of time working on the hydro gravitronic accelerator. Before I knew it, I only had a few minutes to get here," she said as she continued straight towards Bort, who got to his feet.

"Bo(Xoey!)rt!" he exclaimed, throwing his flippers in the air, happy to see her.

She stood in front of him for a moment before dropping a fist on his head, causing him to squish a little. He covered his head with his flippers and stared at Xoey in surprise. "Besides," Xoey began, "I had to run to the market just before getting here." As she slung a pack from her arm, she added in a smoky tone, "I thought I would surprise you with this, dummy," and pulled a brand-new video game from her bag.

Bort's eyes widened, and he shot his flippers from his head to the game. "Bo(Super Adventure Jump Hero RPG II: Curse of the Spooky Spiral Tower! By the Pancakes!)rt!" he gasped, stomping his feet in excitement.

Garlic smiled. "Hey, you've been talking about that game for a few months now, haven't you?" she said as she got to her feet to greet her old friend.

Xoey looked over at Garlic. "Yeah, this dummy wouldn't stop talking about it. Lucky for you, it was the last one they had at Level Up. We should see what all the hype is about tomorrow," she said, trying not to reveal her own excitement. Bort danced around his deck, holding the new video game up above his head. As the pair watched Bort celebrate, Xoey turned to Garlic. "So, what'd I miss?" she asked.

Garlic chuckled then shook her head and lowered it before closing her eyes. "Oh, we were just reminiscing about when we first met," she said, returning Xoey's gaze.

"Oh, that's right. It was about a year ago to the day that you found him in Lemnear," Xoey said.

"Yeah, and he has been able to remember even the smallest details, thank the Golwen gods. So, it's good to know that his amnesia hasn't progressed," Garlic replied.

Xoey made it a point never to show her emotions. But Garlic, knowing her for a long while, knew the subtle clues to look for. A twitch from her antennae was all Garlic needed to see.

"It is good to see him in such high spirits. I remember how sad he looked the first time I laid eyes on him. He'd be unrecognizable now," Xoey said.

Bort froze in his dance and dashed over to Xoey, getting his face close to hers, oblivious to their conversation. "Bo(Hey, hey, hey! Xoey! Before you got here, I was remembering when I first met Garlic, and you know what?)rt?" Bort said with every ounce of enthusiasm in his heart.

"What's that, dummy?" Xoey said with a giggle.

Bort took a step back and trembled with excitement before bounding in the air with the game overhead. "Bo(I remember! I remember! I remember when I met Xoey, too!)rt!" he said with his head held high.

CHAPTER V

No Need for Sorrow

365 DAYS EARLIER

The apothecary was dark, save for a few salt-rock lamps and bioluminescent plants emitting a warm, cozy glow. Potions bubbled over beakers and mystic spell glyphs swirled alongside power stones, Incense wafted down the hall to the only bright room in Garlic's home, where the drone of a bath being drawn could be heard between Bort's muffled sobs.

Bort stood atop a wooden stool wiping his unending tears away, stifling his cries to a whimper. Garlic reached over to a small vial in an ornate wooden box. She glanced over at Bort and hesitated before she pulled from it, a rare bubble-foam elixir. It was a potion, meticulously made with ingredients hard to come by, that reinvigorated the soul and calmed the heart. Best of all, it had a touch of menthol and was scented with eucalyptus. It was Garlic's custom blend, which she called Fenix Foam. She looked over at Bort, seeing him covered in dirt. His skin sagged, drenched from the stream, and he shivered with cold. His eyes welled with tears, and the bright light they held had diminished as they focused inward, searching for lost answers with barren results.

Garlic stood up and

faced Bort. "Okay, mister. This'll make you feel much better," she said and leaned into him with a finger at her face. "I was gonna save this Fenix Foam for a very special occasion for myself, you know," she said. She stood upright, tapping her finger against her chin, and thought hard for a while. She closed her eyes with a sigh, folding her arms, and shook her head. "Hm... But I think you'll need it much more than me," she said with a shrug, finalizing the decision in her mind. Garlic smiled at Bort and pulled the cork from the vial, emptying its contents into the bath, where it fizzed and bubbled up into a cloudy, frothy foam. She then smiled and placed her fists on her hips. "Right. Let's get you in there," she said, nodding her head in the direction of the bath.

Bort watched her, wringing his flippers in front of him. He sniffled with a weak grin before wiping a final tear from his eyes and nodded. "Bort," he acknowledged, and reached out towards Garlic.

Garlic smiled; the emotions that ran through her were oddly pleasant. Her blue eyes gleamed like the azure sky when she bent forward and picked him up. "C'mon, little piggy. Up you go," she said and placed him in the bath.

"Bo(Oooh...)rt..." Bort said, feeling the warmth of the water soak through his body as he lowered into the steamy bubbly water. The magic-infused herbs took effect straightaway. Bort felt his heavy heart lighten and his shattered spirit grow calm. Like melting candle wax dripping into the bath, he relaxed. He closed his eyes, submitting to the feeling and sinking deep into the foamy waters, exposing only a smiling whiskered face surrounded by cloudy white bubbles.

"Bo(Ahh... so nice. So warm...)rt..." Bort mumbled.

Garlic took a seat on the stool and watched him enjoy his bath. Before long, she sat up straight and dropped a fist into her open palm. "Oh! I got something else for you! I'll be right back," she said as she raced out of the bathroom.

"Bo(Okay)rt," Bort said long and drawn out, exposing the tip of his flipper from the foam.

Garlic entered her bedroom and found a little floaty rubber duck donning a wizard's hat. She grabbed him, looking him square in the face. "Okay, Ganduck the Grey. You got a new mission I just know you'll be up for," she said in a playful captain's tone, making her way back to the bathroom.

"I'm sure Bort would love to meet you and..." she said to the rubber duck before slowing her pace as the realization of the situation rooted into her mind. Now that she had found Bort, how was she going to take care of him? What was he going to do? How long would it be? Would it interfere with her work and research? What would the impact of her life be trying to look after him? There were so many questions that entered her mind; it was overwhelming.

Garlic's bout of thoughts was interrupted by the buzzing notification of an incoming call from her living room. Garlic shot a glance into her living room, where the spirits sent the answer to her questions. There was only one other person she thought to seek advice from. With a relieved smile, Garlic walked up to her computer as it blinked. It was Garlic's best and only close friend in Lemnear. A picture displayed a female bee-like being next to the "incoming call" holo-text bubble.

"Hmm... Xoey might know what to do," she said as she reached to answer.

CHAPTER VI

Friends?

"Hey Bort, stay still," Garlic said, laughing, shielding herself from Bort's playful splashes. Garlic sat on the stool with a sponge, trying her best to scrub down the squirming walrus. Bort's mood had taken a radical turn for the better after a long soak, especially now he had a bath-time rubber-ducky-buddy, Ganduck the Grey. Once Garlic placed Ganduck the Grey in the bath next to Bort, his eyes popped open, examining his new companion. His somber feelings washed away like the mud from his body, turning back into the jubilant walrus that bounced off the mushroom pads. Excited to play with his new friend, Bort splashed in the water.

"Bo(Bubbles! Bubbles!)rt!" Bort said, covered in soap suds, waving his flippers in the water with Ganduck the Grey floating nearby casting his happiness spells at the sailing bubbles.

Distracted by the bobbing duck, Bort turned his back to Garlic. Garlic shook the water off that he'd splashed onto her and spotted her chance to scrub his back when she noticed the giant lump on his head. Studying it for a moment, she gingerly put her finger on it, causing Bort to freeze. He shot his flippers up to his bump and spun around to face Garlic with two giant teardrops hanging from his eyes, mouth agape. "Bo(Ow! My owie!)rt!" Bort said.

Garlic sat back. "Hmm… That looks like a serious hit you took there, Bort. I might be able to treat it," she said and reached out to feel it once more.

Bort scuttled away to the far corner of the bath. "Bo(No — ooo…)rt…" he said, trying to hide behind the rubber duck. "Bo(It hurts so bad! It feels like sparks shoot all the way down to my feets when you touch it)rt," he said.

Garlic sat upright and took a long deep breath. Figuring Bort was already frightened, Garlic thought of a gentle way to explain that he needed treatment, and this kind of thing was her specialty. Besides, she wasn't going to let him go to sleep until she knew the severity of the injury. Before she got a chance to explain, a soft knock sounded at her back door facing the alleyway.

The door clicked open. "Hey, Garlic, it's me, Xoey," Xoey exclaimed.

Garlic looked over her shoulder. "Hey! Over here!" she called out while Bort extended his head past Garlic to see who it was, still covering his head with his flippers.

Xoey's gait was delicate, as if she glided across the floor. However, each of her footfalls resounded with heavy thuds. Stepping into the light, she donned a mechanized set of goggles and a pack slung on her back. Now standing in the bathroom doorway, she wore a blue jumpsuit and an eager look on her face.

"Hey, Garlic!"

"Hey, Xoey!"

They greeted one another. Xoey leaned against the doorframe, folding her arms, and cocked her head at Bort. Her antennae twitched as she felt the energy and emotions of the room and from herself. "Whoa! Are you sure he isn't a Wilding?" Xoey said, raising the goggles off her eyes.

"I don't think so. I've never seen anything like him before. But I'm not entirely sure," Garlic said.

Bort's energy signature was incredible, making Xoey's antennae drift around atop her head like stargrass on gusty days. She felt an enormous amount of emotion and potent energy flowing through the little walrus. Never had Xoey felt so much from someone before; it made her head spin. Being a beylan, sensing the shifts in electrostatic energy and emotions was innate, and she was especially preceptive to them. It embarrassed her how severe she was able to sense the emotions from others. It took a lot of work not to internalize them and appear indifferent. Hence, she did her best to either bury them or not be around people with intense emotions. Feeling Bort's herculean energy field was by far the strongest she had ever felt. Xoey tried her best to suppress her empathy, but Bort's emotions were so powerful it made her head throb. Xoey winced and placed a hand on her temple, rubbing it gently.

Bort noticed Xoey's discomfort. "Bo(You have an owie, too?)rt?" he said.

Xoey smiled. "Yeah, something like that," she said.

Bort brought his flippers down to rest on the side of the tub, exposing his head lump. "Bo(I got one, too. See?)rt?" Bort said. "Bo(We're lumpheads!)rt!"

Garlic's jaw fell slack. "Wait... You understood what he said?" Garlic asked.

Xoey smirked and nodded, tapping her head. "Of course! How couldn't you? It's a simple language. Besides, his facial expressions and body language say it all," she said, walking past Garlic. "Besides, I," Xoey emphasized, "am a genius," she sneered, teasing Garlic.

Bort looked over to Garlic. "Bo(Yeah, yeah. She's a genius.)rt," Bort said to Garlic and turned back to Xoey. "Bo(What's a genius?)rt?" he said.

Garlic laughed and waved them off.

Xoey knelt by the side of the tub, still smirking. "I... " she accentuated, "...am a genius! So what's yer name?"

Bort stared at her with pure and earnest eyes. "Bort," he said with the raise of his head, holding onto the edge of the tub.

"Huh, I should've known. Well, it's good to meet'cha, Bort. My name is Xoey Zephyr. That makes us friends now," Xoey said.

Bort jerked back and his eyes darted back and forth, "Bo(F-friends?)rt?" Bort said in a slow and deliberate manner. He felt stinging shockwaves pulse through his head while vague memories and fragmented feelings fired through his mind at lightning speed. Bort held his head, wincing.

Friends? Friends?

The words echoed in his mind, triggering an onslaught of shattered memories that faded quicker than they came. Bort tried holding onto any of the images that bounced around his little brain. He shot up to his feet and began to wring out his flippers. He looked around the room, aware of everything unfamiliar surrounding him, while panic found itself burrowing back into his heart.

"Bo(friends?)rt?" he said. "Bo(Friends… Friends? Friends!)rt," he repeated, each time with increased concern.

"Whoa, what's wrong, Bort?" Xoey said as the wave of Bort's emotional pressure overwhelmed her.

Bort's eyes filled with distress. "Bo(I… I dunno… But I feel… I feel like I need to be looking for someone. Someone really, really important to me…. I feel lost and alone.)rt," Bort said, holding his pounding head.

Garlic looked over to Xoey, who fell speechless. "Who, Bort?" Garlic asked, turning her attention to Bort.

Bort's eyes overflowed with tears. "Bo(I… I dunno… I just… I know that there are people out there I'm not with who I love with all my whole heart. I miss them with every little Bort that I am. I'm so scared…. I don't know… I don't remember… I… I… I…)rt…" Bort said before he became incoherent. Overrun with sadness, Bort covered his face and broke down into a blubbering fit.

Overcome, Xoey had no chance to build a barrier from his emotions. Xoey clenched her teeth, fighting her own tears back. Struggling to swallow back her feelings, she forced them down and grew calm. Xoey closed her eyes and brought a fist to her mouth. "Ahem," she coughed, clearing her throat and at the same time shot Garlic a glance, hoping she hadn't seen her face flush red with the hot wash of embarrassment of losing control of her composure.

Xoey made sure to avoid situations like these. Facing it now without being able to prepare made her panic. She boiled with fury and worry. Unsure what to do, Xoey got to her feet, reeled her fist overhead, and brought it down on Bort's head. "Dummy!" she shouted as she hit him.

Bort squished from the impact which flipped a switch inside him and stopped his crying. His face filled with surprise and shock as he slapped his flippers over his head for cover and stared deep into Xoey's eyes in complete silence.

Xoey reared back with the same look of shock and surprise across her face. Her knee-jerk reaction to Bort's powerful emotions made her panic, answering with a hammer-fist to Bort's noggin. However, what she really wanted to do was comfort her alone and scared new friend. But to her, showing those emotions would be worse than death.

"W-we're f-friends… okay, d-dummy? So, w-we'll help you out. Geez," Xoey said, turning her flush-red face away. It was rare to hear Xoey speak with such benevolence. Even more unusual when she blushed.

Besides being astonished by Xoey's unusual reaction, Garlic resonated with Xoey's feelings concerning their new strange little friend. "Y-yeah, Bort, don't worry. We're your friends too. So, we can help you," Garlic said.

Bort looked at them both with his flippers covering his head and his wrinkled brow relaxed. Their words felt whole and genuine. Believing them, his swirling thoughts began to calm. The thought of having Garlic and Xoey as friends made Bort happy; really happy. The creases on his forehead moved to the sides of his eyes and mouth as a weak smile grew on his face.

"Bo("My… friends?)rt?" Bort said.

Garlic smiled. "Of course we're friends, Bort," Garlic said.

"Yeah, we're friends, too, even though you're a big dummy" Xoey said.

Bort trusted them, and his weak smile grew sincere. As he looked between his two new friends, when his eyes returned to Xoey, something stood out to him. To his surprise, he was able to meet Xoey face to face. Bort looked back at Garlic, who was so much taller than he was. Annoyed at being so short, he glowered at Garlic and turned back to Xoey, who, on the contrary…

Bort tilted his head, his expression softened and he examined Xoey closer with great interest. Already uncomfortable from exposing her 'affectionate' side, Xoey drew back, blushed a deeper red from Bort's piercing gaze, and her heart pounded in her chest. "Wha… What?" Xoey said in a harsh and defensive tone.

Bort traced an imaginary dotted line from the top of her head back to him. Could it be he was just a smidge taller?

"Bo(Hey!)rt!" Bort exclaimed and threw his flippers in the air, forgetting his deep sorrow.

Xoey and Garlic flinched in surprise.

He put his flipper to his head and matched it with Xoey's height, repeating the movement back and forth a few times. "Bo(Look! Look! I am a little taller than you!)rt!" he said.

Xoey's empathy drained from her face and twisted into one of boiling anger, while Garlic doubled over laughing. If there was one thing Xoey despised, it was that she was so short. With a bit more commitment behind her fist this time, she gave Bort another first-class ticket aboard the Knuckle Express.

Smack!

Bort squished again and covered his head in shock as Xoey stared at him with fury in her eyes. "Dummy! Look harder!" she said and pointed a finger up. Bort kept his flippers on his head while his gaze followed her finger. Her antennae! They were almost a whole foot taller than him! If you added the crest of her windswept hair to this factor, her height came up just above Garlic's shoulders. Xoey turned her face up and away from Bort. "Hmph. Besides, you're standing in the tub! That's two extra inches at least," she barked and folded both sets of arms.

Begrudgingly, Bort relented to the fact that he was still the shortest. He contorted his face and plopped back down into the bath with his arms folded. "Bo(Argh! Just you wait! I'm gonna grow up so much! I'm gonna be ginormous! More ginormouser than both of you! Hmph!)rt!" Bort said, exaggerating his size with his flippers before turning his attention back to playing with the bubbles and Ganduck the Grey, while Garlic held her stomach, pained from her fit of laughter.

"A dummy like you could never be taller than a genius like me," Xoey said.

Bort looked at Xoey and covered his head. "Bo(Because you're cheating! You keep squishing me shorter by hitting my brain meats!)rt," Bort said.

"Oh, put a sock in it, will ya, dummy?" Xoey said.

Bort smirked. "Bo(Hmm, joke's on you. I happen to love socks.)rt," Bort said. He closed his eyes and turned his head up and away, feeling smug and witty. Xoey stared at the content walrus, who sat in a bubble bath next to a floating rubber ducky. His comeback was more than enough to make her like him. She snorted and burst into laughter.

Bort felt the anguish of his spirit unwind. Maybe it was the frustration of realizing how tiny he was, or from Xoey's dome-duster, or perhaps it was from the healing effects of the Fenix Foam and Ganduck the Grey. But it was more likely from how happy it made him to know he made such good friends so soon, and his short attention span. Either way, Bort couldn't help but follow in their laughter alongside his two new friends.

CHAPTER VII

Bort is Bort!

Fifteen minutes later, Bort emerged from the bath smelling fragrant and squeaky clean. The only problem was that towels did not dry him thoroughly. Xoey and Garlic thought maybe hanging him out to dry would be good. But he would have to be there for a long time, and he squirmed like a worm. Plus, it was nighttime, and he'd probably be freezing throughout the night. After pulling him down from the clothesline, they tried hair dryers while shaking him to dry, which only made him feel hot and dizzy. The pair thought about it for a while, before they looked over to the laundry-room dryer. They looked back at one another and shrugged.

Tumbling in the dryer became one of Bort's new favorite things. His happy face spun round and round as he looked out the dryer window. Bort snorted and giggled, seeing Garlic and Xoey's concerned faces stare in at him spin from his perspective.

Ding!

The dryer played its melody, signaling the end of the dry cycle. Garlic and Xoey looked to one another, before Garlic opened the door. A giant puffball, Bort floated out, slow and elegant like a dandelion seed drifting in the wind.

"Bo(Whoa...)r..." Bort said, amazed. His eyes darted left, right, and then down. He flailed his flippers in the air as the air current tumbled him in somersaults. Bort began laughing. The feeling of sailing through the room was exhilarating. Lost in his own world, he barely heard Garlic and Xoey's panicked screams. They jumped, reaching frantic hands that grazed his fluff, desperately trying to get him back on the ground. Bort's laughter switched to a groan of disappointment as Xoey finally caught one of his fluttering flippers, and he sailed down, with one foot tied to a string, and the other to Xoey's wrist, where he floated over her like a balloon.

After Bort was brushed off and looking like a spiffy new walrus, Xoey sat him in Garlic's living room, where she put her goggles on and began to examine him.

"Hmm..." she mumbled, replacing her goggles atop her head. "Well, he's positively not a Wilding," she said.

Garlic was preparing some herbs and salves to tend to his wound. "Yeah, that's what I thought... So, what is he?" Garlic asked, looking over her shoulder.

Bort looked over at them. "Bo(I am a Bort! I am a good-boy Bort.)rt," he said with an angelic expression.

Garlic walked over to him carrying a bowl of salve, some water, a towel, gauze, herbs, and a few potions. "Okay then, good-boy Bort, let's have a look at that bump," Garlic said while Xoey brought her goggles down, looking into his eyes with an ophthalmoscope.

Bort gasped and warily covered his lump. "Bo(Just kidding! I'm a bad-boy Bort.)rt," he said, scowling, trying to look criminal.

Garlic sighed. "All right, tough guy, let's have a look," she said, calling his miserable bluff.

Bort dropped the act out of fear, seeing that Garlic was serious as she walked towards him. "Bo(N-no w-wait!)rt!" he stammered, and tried to run away, interrupting Xoey's examination.

"Oh, no, you don't," Garlic said as she sped over to him, grabbing his flippers. Xoey pulled her goggles back to her head, revealing a face filled with annoyance as she backed away and searched for other tools to continue the examination, providing Garlic time to wrestle and restrain him.

"Bo(Ah! No! I dun wanna! I dun—)r—" was all Bort was able to get out before Garlic restrained him and swiftly applied a towel dipped in Arctic Hyssop extract to clean his wound. "Sorry, this'll sting a bit," Garlic said, wrapping her legs around Bort, pinning his flippers.

"Bo(N-no! Wait!)rt!" Bort cried before Garlic placed the towel on his wound. His eyes went blank, and pain jolted through his body. Fragmented, garbled memories flashed through his mind as his vision went white and his ears began to ring.

"Bort!" Bort yelped. It felt like hot lava was poured over his head. He struggled like a flopping fish in Garlic's legs, which clamped him like a vice.

The terrible sensation doubled. "Just bear with me a little more, Bort," Garlic said and reached for her ice-flower salve.

"Bo(No more! I give up! I give up! Tap! Tap!)rt!" he squealed, while Garlic rubbed the salve over the bump with tender and experienced hands.

Bort strained his eyes closed. "Bo(Wai— Oh...)rt..." he screamed before cutting it short. The ice-flower salve felt cool and healing; plus, it smelled nice. Bort popped his eyes open. His vision started to return, albeit with a few spots, and the ringing in his ears began to fade. The intensity of the pain was dropping as the hot lava cooled and numbed. Bort stopped struggling and closed his eyes as his head buzzed. It felt terrific as Garlic applied the salve with a scalp massage.

"See?" Garlic said in a dulcet tone, releasing her lockdown on Bort. "You gotta trust me."

Bort mumbled, "Bo(Ahh... you're so nice. The bestest. A genius.)rt," and re-laxed into Garlic as she cared for him while Xoey ran a device over Bort, continuing her examination.

Time passed, and Garlic kept tending to Bort's injury as Xoey now held a stethoscope to his chest. Xoey hummed and pulled the stethoscope off her ears, placing it on her lap, where Bort picked it up as soon as she put it down; as he did with each tool she used on him. Bort fiddled with it a moment before figuring out how to use it, and he mimicked Xoey's examination on her.

"So?" Garlic said as she wrapped Bort's head.

Bort studied the stethoscope before placing it over Xoey's stomach. He squinted and listened. His eyes popped wide open at the peculiar sounds he heard from Xoey's body, before moving the stethoscope over her ribs and back, whereupon his eyes grew even wider.

Xoey, ignored Bort's examination and explained her findings. "It is completely unfounded. Bort is absolutely not a Wilding, but he isn't Keevahling either." Xoey folded her lower arms. She outstretched her upper arms, placed them behind her head, and leaned back in her seat. Bort continued his examination by moving the stethoscope over Xoey's heart while she said, "It's like..." Xoey hesitated, shaking her head.

"Like what?" Garlic asked, looking up at her.

Xoey looked over at Garlic. "It's like he is not even real... Like he is a toy or something." She paused. "But that is impossible... right?" she said, hoping that asking aloud would provide the answer somehow.

"A toy?" Garlic repeated, surprised. She looked at the used gauze covered in small dabs of blood. "Are you sure?" she asked in disbelief.

Xoey shook her head. "I can hear his lungs, his heart, the grumbles in his stomach, and feel his pulse through his body.... However, his skin feels like a blanket, but it is warm. He feels soft like cotton but firm like sinew when he moves. He speaks, thinks, has his own feelings and thoughts, but looks stitched together," she said.

Xoey snapped her head forward. "There is one last test," she said and held her hand out in front of her in Bort's direction. On her forearm was a device that began to whir and glow. Appearing from the atmosphere, small shielding and glowing particles swirled around her. "Assuming control," she commanded.

Xoey's hair flowed, and energetic winds whirled around the room. Garlic held onto her hat, and Bort continued to listen to Xoey's chest, unfazed. Soon, everything calmed, and the swirling winds settled.

Xoey brought her hand back down. "Well, my technomancy had no effect. So, he isn't a droid, or cyborg, or anything mechanical," Xoey said.

"Huh, I guess Bort really is just Bort," Garlic said, finishing up bandaging

Bort's noggin and washing her hands.

"That is the logical conclusion," Xoey said, forcing out the inconclusive answer.

Bort brought the stethoscope off his ears, stared at the floor, and shook his head. With a deep sigh, he looked up into Xoey's eyes. "Bo(You have a case of the tick-tocks in the chest, I'm afraid. And windies in your back. You also have monsters in your tummy. It all looks grim.)rt," Bort said, pretending to know what he was talking about.

CHAPTER VIII

Happy Birthday, Bort

BACK TO PRESENT DAY

Garlic and Xoey listened to Bort recall the memory as they sat at the edge of Castle Bort, leaning on the rails with their feet dangling in the air. Bort sat between the two, gazing into the exploding sky, which billowed into different colors, and kicked his legs. Xoey smiled as her mind took her back to that day. "I can't believe it has already been a year. It only feels like you showed up a few months ago," she said.

"Yeah, Bort," Garlic said. "Time feels like it has flown by. But at the same time, I feel like I met you ages ago."

"Bo(It's like my birthday!)rt!" Bort said.

"Hey! That's a wonderful idea! We can use the Lifestream as your birthday!" Garlic said with a beaming smile and clasping her hands together in excitement.

"Then, I am glad I brought you a little birthday gift, dummy," Xoey said with a laugh.

"Happy birthday, Bort!" Garlic said and hugged him.

"Yeah, happy birthday," Xoey echoed with a playful punch to his arm.

Bort's eyes lit up with a bright smile while he rubbed his shoulder. He couldn't remember when or where he was born. But to have a birthday during such a wonderful event made him really happy. More importantly, he would be sure to always remember it. The three friends watched the sky once more in silence as Xoey ran her hand over the woodwork of the treehouse.

"Hey, I remember when we helped you build Castle Bort," Xoey said. "Before that, every night as the sun set, you'd always be sitting on Oak Tree Hill in my backyard, dreaming up into the sky."

"Bo(That's when I asked you about space.)rt," Bort said in a loud whisper, spreading his flippers to the sky.

Garlic laughed and leaned over the railing to look at Xoey. "Ha-ha! Wasn't he there yesterday?" Garlic said.

Xoey looked at Garlic and giggled. "If Bort isn't there every night, it's every other. Always asking me about space," Xoey said.

Bort smiled. Bo(I like to go there after getting ingredients for pancakes! Space is so cool!)rt!" he said, keeping his flippers outstretched.

Xoey looked at him before giving him a soft shoulder check. "Well... It's never a bother. You're welcome any time, you hear?" she said with unexpected aggression. "You can ask me all you want about space, too." She yelled and fidgeted with embarrassment. Xoey turned her face away, flustered, never wanting Bort to stop visiting her.

"Speaking of pancakes, Bort, do you remember the day you tore my kitchen apart? I was so angry with you. You were covered in flour, and there was syrup and cream everywhere," Garlic said.

"Bo(I remember that. I made lots of stinky clouds that day too.)rt," Bort said, bursting with confidence.

Reliving that moment, Garlic laughed and shot her head back. "Ugh! Don't remind me! There's still a faint scent of burnt pancakes in the kitchen," she groaned.

"Ha-ha, yeah, but that was the first time we'd ever had what he calls pancakes. They were nothing like I'd ever had," Xoey said, defending Bort, and continued the story. Her experience had been far more positive. "My nutrition condenser was low, and I was starving. I came over hoping you'd have something to eat. My wish came true, seeing plates of food lain out on the table. They looked so weird. I thought you'd bombed another dish! I wanted to ask you what they were, but you were tearing Bort a new one," Xoey said.

"Wha—? Hey!" Garlic, offended, interrupted Xoey's story.

"Face it, Garlic, cooking was never your strong suit," Xoey said with a shrug.

Garlic folded her arms and pouted. "That may be so, but you're no better! You use a nutrition condenser!"

Xoey hummed, folding her upper arms. She propped herself up with her lower limbs and looked to the sky. "Okay, cooking was never our strongest suit," Xoey corrected.

Garlic huffed and groaned. "Yeah."

"Bo(I love pancakes!)rt!" Bort said.

Xoey continued her story. "Anyway, those pancakes smelled so good, I couldn't help myself and dug in. I was so hungry." Her antennae twitched, and a slight smile showed on her face. "Even though that was so long ago, I can still taste them to this day."

Garlic couldn't disagree with that. "You're right. Once I calmed down and tried those pancakes, they were otherworldly," she sighed as they both rested their chins on their hands and looked off with longing expressions.

Bort lived with Garlic for the first few months in Lemnear and, before long, displayed his skills as a great chef. Because of his amnesia, he couldn't recall why he loved making food, but he always found himself drawn to the kitchen. Bort could create many delicious meals, but explicitly enjoyed making circular culinary cuisines, with pancakes being his specialty.

However, there was one dark side to Bort when it came to food experimentation. After finding a unique flavor or finishing a new dish, Bort needed to taste what the exact opposite of delicious was. So, every now and then, he would go out of his way to concoct some of the most atrociously foul-tasting meals. His favorite test subject was himself, which yielded many varying results, from spending full days on the toilet, to sometimes being felled unconscious for days. Still, he would rope Garlic and Xoey into tasting his new "wonders", as he so fondly referred to them.

Across the region of Lemnear and beyond, pancakes were unheard of. Inevitably, word got out that a mysterious stranger made exquisite, never-before-seen dishes called pancakes at the apothecary. Garlic's clinic soon doubled as an eatery. It didn't take long until most of the townspeople were pleading for Bort to open a restaurant. Luck had it that the old, arcane magical-rune shop had moved into the secret hollow-grove district and remained vacant. It was a home burrowed out of an ancient sequoia stump with a few living branches that had since sprouted. It was conveniently located between Garlic and Xoey's houses. Soon after, Bort hung his own Pancake Shop sign over his new house, along with all the curious things he found interesting to decorate it. Because it was an old mystical shop, Bort found plenty of unwanted surprises while cleaning it out. To this day, there are cupboards he has not used that might contain bat wings or mysterious skulls.

"Bo(But you guys can eat them anytime you want, sillies!)rt!" Bort said.

"Well, yeah, but… Every time feels like the first time, and those first ones will always be the first ones," Xoey said.

"Couldn't have put it better myself," Garlic said.

"Bo(Come for breakfast tomorrow. I'll save some counter seats for you guys.) rt," Bort said with a toothy grin.

Garlic stood up and stretched. "You know I won't turn that down. Well, it's getting late. I better head back now if I am going to be up early enough to get breakfast," she said and gave a thumbs-up. Garlic grabbed Ashgrowl, sprinted to the edge of the deck and jumped off, throwing Ashgrowl to her feet. "Las!" she commanded. Ashgrowl kicked into life and positioned itself under Garlic's boots. Ashgrowl absorbed her fall like a hydraulic shock before its crystal lit up and they took off towards Garlic's house. As she sped off, Garlic exclaimed from just within earshot, "Don't stay up too late, Bort!"

Xoey pulled her goggles down from her head. "I better do the same," she said before turning to Bort with a warning finger in front of his face. "Now, don't you play that game without me. Let's play it together tomorrow," she said before she too jumped off the deck, spreading her wings and fluttering to her domain.

"Bo(See ya later!)rt!" Bort said, waving.

Once they were out of sight, Bort felt delighted to be able to spend his one-year anniversary, which he now called his birthday, with his two close friends. Bort stared up into the sky a bit longer, letting his imagination be whisked away into the Lifestream. Everything about the night felt so wonderful, so why did he feel apprehension grow inside his belly? The uneasiness had begun when he'd recounted his memories to Garlic and Xoey. But each time he sensed them, Bort shook the feeling off and explained it away as having an upset tummy or that his brain had gotten overcooked. But this seed had rooted in the depths of his heart. Now that he was alone with only himself for company, that silent whisper grew, and bona fide dissatisfaction washed over him.

Bort's expression grew sullen. How could anything be wrong? he thought. The night was pure, and the heavens were terrific. But the longer Bort gazed off, dreaming, to the stars, that uneasiness crept in and grew. Bort's eyelids began to grow heavy, and he crawled into the nest of pillows and blankets to retire for the night.

CHAPTER IX

Racing the Sun towards the Dawn of a New Day

Beep, beep, beep!

A small alarm clock chirped, and two small legs extended out from the bottom of it before it stood up. The feet to the clock marched in place accompanied by the sounds of mechanisms engaging. The alarm first paraded around a large pile of blankets that began to undulate. Once the clock sensed movement, it ran in circles and jumped with every chime of its bell, excited to be doing its job.

From within the heap, Bort grumbled, then tossed and turned. A single flipper slithered out from the blankets and slapped for the alarm. The alarm clock's programming initiated and dodged it, seeing Bort's flipper coming a mile away. Each of Bort's attempts to push the snooze button quickened, as the clock's movements became more nimble. Growing annoyed, Bort's frantic flails struck with intent, and the desire to press the snooze button turned into trying to smash it. Pausing , Bort faked left, then right, and caught the clock midair. Outsmarting the alarm, Bort flipped the disarm switch and set the clock facedown on the deck where his flipper snaked back into the nest of blankets.

Each night Bort decided to sleep in his treehouse, he would make a mental note to exchange the alarm clock for something less... Infuriating. But every morning after shutting it off, the mental note fled into the vault of his to-do lists, where a vast stack of other notes ended up. Such as attempting to eat a kidney bean again, and, of course, to study the smells of his feet.

Bort rolled onto his back, threw his flippers out in front of him, and sat straight up like a zombie rising from the grave. With half-closed, sleepy eyes, he stretched up into the sky with a mighty lion-like yawn. After, Bort smacked his lips and scratched his chest. He plopped back down, brought his knees to his chest, and kip-upped to his feet.

"Bort. Bor-Bort!" Bort sang out, greeting the morning. With some light stretches, a few squats, and running in place, he primed himself to tackle a new day. Bort walked up to the edge of Castle Bort, where he was met by a single waking sunbeam. Bort closed his eyes and raised his head to the sky as it dusted with sunrays that felt good on his whiskered face. Through the patches of clouds where the heavens were still dark, the end of the Lifestream was still visible through the peaking daylight.

Bort took in a deep breath, exhaled, and opened his eyes. For him, the mystery of the night wove adventures both frightening and wonderous, but the mornings were beloved most of all. Not only did he love waking up before the Sun, but it was the start of a brand-new day, a brand-new adventure. Bort smiled and cracked his flippers. Racing the sunrise was one of his favorite games, eager to spearhead the day before it had a chance to start.

He gazed down at the village below; the vantage from Castle Bort made the town look like a miniature toy playset. Bort bounced in place a few times before he spun around and walked over to an engine with a hand crank on it. After he turned the crank a few times, the machine sputtered before coming alive, and a range of revolving belts, pulleys, and hooks carrying galvanized buckets began moving. There were no stairs or ladders that led to Castle Bort, only this contraption.

Bort hopped inside one of the pails. It swayed a few times while ascending higher into the trees. Bort stuck his face out of the bucket and held on to the rim, bouncing in his excitement. The hook-and-pulley system raised him onto a conveyor belt containing a slide of rollers. A latch disengaged and deposited Bort onto the slide, where his weight moved him forward and gained momentum. Looking over the edge, Bort saw the drop coming that would send him on a roller coaster ride that ran among the trunks and branches of the giant sequoias of Lemnear. With a gleeful bort, he flew through the treetops faster and faster, shooting through the canopy that would deposit him at his house and pancake shop.

Bort descended deeper into the trees, where the morning sun had not yet penetrated. But the glow of lights through stained-glass windows of homes built into the side of the trees painted an array of colors against the forest backdrop. The wind and watermills turned while a few dwellings billowed smoke from their chimneys. Bort's homemade ride took him on a swift tour through Lemnear, where he passed by the warmth of lights from homes and enjoyed the wafting smells of the bakeries making their breads.

Reaching the end of its track, the pail swooped up a ramp, sending Bort out of the bucket and sailing through the air, while it latched back onto the revolving hook-and-pulley system. Bort splayed his flippers out, and from the ground, his silhouette looked like a majestic dragon soaring in the sky. He extended his flippers in front of him and caught a zip line, his home now in sight. The zip line hit the end, sending Bort twisting and flipping toward a padded landing bay. At the last moment, he turned himself into a Bort-cannonball and landed, whereupon he bounced and rolled to a stop.

Bort made his way through his landing pad, which he'd designed to look like his favorite big mech-cartoon, Gun-Tekk. Approaching the door to his house, he had a mock computer display with a control pad to unlock the door. Each button he hit sounded like a different animal noise, and with the correct entry, the doors opened to the Gun-Tekk intro song.

Bort made his way through his home and down to the restaurant floor, glad for taking extra time the day before to prep for the morning rush. It gave him time to work on something he had dreamt of doing since hearing the tales of the pirate warrior, Commander Lemnear Risai T'Leia, while living with Garlic. Since then, Bort looked up to her as his role model.

The accounts of Lemnear Risai T'Leia state that she was responsible for the beginning of the Virtinnore Rebellion, or the Fallen War, as it was commonly referred to in the history books of Keevah. Bort was so captivated by her that he had pictures throughout his restaurant depicting her life, voyages, adventures, and battles. Even in front of his kitchen prep table, Bort had a replicated painting of her that he looked to for motivation and inspiration when he cooked. More importantly, the picture served as a reminder of what he felt he indeed was. Instilled deep within his soul and heart of hearts was the spirit of an adventurer and Bort's true calling. Bort admired the painting and smiled. "Bo(Today is the day.)rt," he said to himself as he touched the canvas, as he did every day before leaving his house. Bort grabbed the pack he'd set out for himself the night before, took one last look at the painting, smiled, and headed out the door.

Bort made sure to leave his 'Back soon!' sign out on his entryway before making his way to the Watertail Plaza Slug-Lug Express stop to catch the first bus to lake Lemnear. There, Bort had been working on a small boat that he had been building ever since he had heard the epic adventures of Lemnear traveling across the lands. She voyaged over turbulent seas and fought with tyrannical beasts and monsters of legend alongside her battle brethren. To the rest of the continent, she was a pirate, a scoundrel, and even a mercenary. To this day, there remain many mixed feelings about who Lemnear really was. But to the townspeople of Lemnear, she was a hero. Her whole beginning started in the town Bort had found himself.

Bort recounted the many tales of Lemnear, as he did every morning he set to work on his boat. The days of Lemnear, millennia ago, was a time wrought with powerful and giant creatures, mutant beasts known as Ulban by the people but self-referred to as the Ainalie. They conquered lands and raided townships that dotted the world, all in the name of their holy belief that the world and all who inhabited it where specifically for their control and knew no better.

The Ulban armies were vast, and their power unmatched. They accumulated strength through force and taking everything from the people, from their goods and resources to their weapons and technology. After they razed cities, the Ulban enslaved those who were fit enough to work, calling it a blessing to serve the chosen. Those deemed unfit for labor were killed; explaining away as mercy for the suffering. Those who stood defiant were branded heretics, made examples of, and killed.

In Lemnear's era, at a young age, she was taught to bend at the knee and give the Ulban everything. When she could take it no more, she stood to her feet and resisted. As punishment, she was to watch her parents murdered before her and become a young bride to their lowest ranks. In her shock and despair, she was seized by the Ulban and treated as property. But like a smoldering flame deep within her heart, her courage grew, and just as they set sail, she again, defied them. Being younger, smaller, and weaker, she used every tactic she could. Sometimes she would poison food, lure drunken Ulban overboard, or prompt infighting.

The others who were captured along with her saw the Ulban become demoralized at Lemnear's tactics and became emboldened and joined her cause. In due course, a mutiny was orchestrated, where Lemnear, others enslaved, and even a few Ulban who'd pledged their fealty to Lemnear, overtook the ship, and battle descended on the Ulban fleet. Each vessel they raided bolstered Lemnear's ranks, as each ship containing prisoners revolted and became her crew.

Years later, at the end of the Fallen War, Lemnear returned to her hometown. Hereafter the records of Lemnear become obscure with many unreliable stories of her life after the war. Some believed that her bloodlust continued and started the underbelly syndicate known as the Nameless. Others say her fame in the uprisings got her murdered by the jealous and vengeful. Different accounts told of Lemnear's remorse for collapsing the Ainalie Empire, dismantling the law and order of the time, and ensuing the terrifying reality of freedom.

Unable to cope, she lived the rest of her life as a hermit atop the Spiral Cliffs. Some say she wandered Keevah as a spectral vagrant, but the majority believed that in her troubled life, she found a small measure of peace and tranquility, discovering a long-sought-after love where she was able to accept the despair of her past, heal her wounded soul, and lived out the rest of her days rebuilding her hometown, which, in the end, was renamed in her honor.

Bort knew the tales of every possible fate she could have come across and had read them countless times. Yet, Bort was one of the few that believed they had all happened to her, but the one he liked the most was the one where she found love and peace. In the time Bort spent in Lemnear, he had learned that Lemnear was a village founded resolutely on freedom and the choice to become what you desired to be, unrestricted by governing limitations on currency. The village had adopted the principles of self-sovereignty based on individuals voluntarily coexisting in a community and each caring for one another. All for one, and one for all.

However, no matter which of Lemnear's outcomes people believed, everyone was sure of one thing: once the fighting was over, Lemnear would have travelled across the lake that Bort would soon be standing on the shores of and scaled the Spiral Cliffs that jutted out from the middle of the lake high into the sky, shrouded with misty clouds. She'd scaled to the top and laid her sword, Glimmering Sparrow, to watch over the world as the protector that he, the sword, was. Over the eons, the story of the mighty warrior, Lemnear, became a fairy tale to tell to kids before bedtime, and had been changed to fit the times. As the tales became muddled with different versions, Lemnear was still held in high regard by the elders of the town and filled the minds of children with dreams of adventure. Yet, for many of the adults, it was only an old tale. A statue of Lemnear and her crew had been erected in the middle of Watertail Plaza long ago by an unknown artist. There, kids could be found pretending to be on the same adventures Lemnear had found herself on, while the elderly paid respects, offered prayers, and bestowed gifts, especially around the Lifestream holiday.

For as long as Bort could remember, which, alas, was not too long ago, he had always dreamt of adventure and exploration. Bort wanted desperately to be like the heroes Garlic had read to him about in the books he found in her library. Even before coming to Lemnear, Bort felt in his heart of hearts that adventure called to him. Convinced, he believed that the quickest way to become an adventurer would be to build a boat, set sail for the Spiral Cliffs, ascend the treacherous cliff face that not even airships can reach, and seek out Lemnear's Glimmering Sparrow.

Bort would often collect any materials he was offered or found at the market, or found by scouring the lakeside for anything useful during his free time, all in hopes of building his ship and setting sail just like Lemnear had done long, long ago. Today was no exception. Bort was offered some used rope at the lakeside marina and was eager to add it to his vessel. It was the last thing needed to test his boat's seaworthiness!

The bus rang its bells, announcing the final boarding before departure. Bort scrambled into the bus and took his seat, bouncing with eagerness and plastering his face against the window. The ride time to the lake was about ten minutes, but Bort's excitement made each minute drag on like hours.

CHAPTER X

Good

Bort took a deep breath in and exhaled. "Bo(Ahh… The smell of smells in the morning.)rt, "Bort said and disembarked. He beelined for the marina, where one of the storekeepers had left a coil of rope out for him. Bort took the rope and exchanged it with a pack of premade lunches. Bort carried the spool through the harbor shops and followed the shoreline to a small outcropping of rocks where his boat was. Bort smiled, dropped the rope, and pulled out a piece of paper that contained the precious blueprints of his ship that he made using his favorite crayons. It depicted a mighty vessel, along with Bort as its captain, hook-hand and all, waving with gusto. Bort nodded, adhering to his plans, and stowed the paper away, only to reveal a hodgepodge of wood, cloth, rusty metal, and bandages that were his ship.

To anyone else, the boat looked less than seaworthy. The mere fact it had been withstanding the gentle winds that lapped over the lake was already a feat.

But to Bort, it was the most beautiful, well-built, fantastic ship he had ever set eyes on. Bort poured his blood, sweat, and tears into building his vessel, hoping to one day voyage as Lemnear had and search for the Glimmering Sparrow.

Bort cocked his head and reflected on his work. There were people in the town who had greater skills than he did, but this was something he felt he needed to do on his own, just like Lemnear had. ...But fighting off a horde of ancient, mutant Ulban beasts sounded scary. Though, for all he knew, they were all gone by now. So, the next-best thing was for him to research and build a boat he could command for himself!

Minutes later, Bort tied the last barrel to his boat with a satisfying clank and wiped the sweat from his brow. He admired his work and erupted into a three-second celebratory dance. After all this time, Bort was ready to test his ship! Since he always seemed to get hungry when he worked, Bort rightfully christened it, Hot Dog. He reached into his pack, procuring a syrup-covered pancake he then slapped to the hull of the boat. Watching it slide down, Bort nodded with a firm, "Bort," making it official. With a twinkle in his eye, Bort shoved off and watched Hot Dog splash into the lake. Seeing it float over the pristine waters, Bort ingrained his dream, now accomplished, deep into his brain meats. Admiring it a moment longer, he then dove into the lake and headed for Hot Dog.

Once aboard, Bort raised the flag he'd meticulously stitched together with his own two flippers. The words Sea Bort was crossed out, but on the bottom, it read, Hot Dog. It was complemented with a crude drawing of a chili-cheese hot dog as its symbol. Bort officially captained Hot Dog on their first voyage.

"Bo(Ahh, so this is what she felt like.)rt," Bort said, imagining being just like Lemnear. Standing at the helm, Bort stared straight ahead over the vast sea — err, lake — before him.

Bort raised his head to the sky. Bathing in the warmth of the early sunlight, he closed his eyes and for a moment was pure and present. His mind was empty, focused on nothing but the experience. Not long after, heavy footfalls approached Bort, and he felt a gentle hand on his shoulder. Aye, it's incredible, isn't it Bort? an omnipotent feminine voice echoed in his mind's eye.

If there was anything other than cooking Bort excelled at, it would be his powerful imagination. Bort had created what Lemnear was undoubtedly like through the tales he had read, and through his own interpretation of what he believed her to be. Whenever he felt alone, or was excited, or even when he was sad and afraid, he always had the characters he'd created in his imagination to talk to. Best of all, they all shared an equal love of slugs to snack on and enjoy alongside him. Lemnear, however, was one of the few that felt as real as he did.

"Bo(Yeah...)rt..." Bort said with an accomplishing sigh.

Ya done good, captain. I'm proud of ye, Lemnear said.

Bort hummed and nodded.

Did ye name her?

"Bo(Hot Dog!)rt."

Did ye remember to raise yer flag?

"Bo(Aye!)rt!"

Aye, good lad. Is the slug container aboard?

Bort pointed to his right at a rustic steel pale. "Bo(Onboard and at the ready.) rt," he said.

Ah! We will have a grand bounty! Lemnear said.

Bort nodded with a determined, "Bort!"

Hmm... and how about the pool? Lemnear asked.

Hearing Lemnear ask such an odd question brought him back to the present. Pool? What pool? Bort felt the warmth of Lemnear dash away and the sensation of a hand on his shoulder, vanish. Bort popped his eyes open and was met with the beautiful mountain-lake backdrop and the sounds of the water lapping against the hull. Already wet, Bort hadn't noticed he was standing in ankle-deep water that sloshed around as the boat rocked. Bort looked down at his feet before putting a flipper to his tusk and crumpling his brow.

That's strange. I don't remember designing a pool on Hot Dog...

Bort shrugged. He could have easily forgotten. But to be sure, he decided to consult the blueprint again.

After duly noting that there indeed was no design for a pool in his plans, Bort looked up, and the severity of the situation fell on him like a ton of kidney beans. In his peripheral, Bort noticed a giant geyser spewing lake water onboard.

"Bort!" Bort cursed as he pounced on the waterspout like a cat catching a mouse. To his right, a knot in the wood vibrated before popping out into the air like a cork. A short-lived geyser erupted before Bort made short work of it with his left flipper, while another rumble and pop came from behind him. Looking over his shoulder, he stretched out his leg and covered it as another burst of water broke through. Bort grunted in frustration before slapping his last free flipper over it. Everything remained silent for a moment before the wood of the ship groaned, and a sickening gurgle came from just in front of Bort. Two bubbling springs of water spewed onto Hot Dog. By the luck of the pancakes, they were far apart enough for him to plug them with his tusks.

Bort lay out flat on the deck of his boat as he literally held the boat together. The ship rocked in the lake with the water lapping against the hull in the gentle breeze. He smiled, thinking the worst was over and figured the damage wasn't so bad. But his relief came too soon, as the vessel creaked. Cracking wood was soon followed by burbling pools, and water jets spewed all around him, dashing his confidence.

With a silent swear, Bort hopped to his feet and grabbed the slug container to use as his only hope to keep his ship from sinking. In a scramble, He bailed water as fast as he could, but Hot Dog's fate was already sealed, as it descended lower into the drink, submitting to the watery depths of the beach a few meters from shore. Relenting to the fact that he would not be able to keep up with the sinking ship, Bort jumped into the water and pushed the boat with all his might to dry land. Once it rested on the shallow sands, he pulled it the rest of the way with a rope that dangled from the raft.

After pulling the ship away from the edge of the water, Bort collapsed on the sandy shore, gasping and wheezing, with the hammering of his heart in his ears. Bort rolled onto his back, flippers outstretched, staring into the cerulean sky, and all became still. The songs of skreigulls in the air, the lapping water, and the melodies of the wind through the trees was profound, and stood out in Bort's awareness.

The breeze blew over Bort, and his wet body cooled the warm sands underneath him. The rhythmic sound of a crab scuttling across the beach caught his attention, and he watched it wander towards Hot Dog, piqued as to what it could be. The little crab crawled over the hull and stopped at the mast, where it bobbed up and down, examining the wood before inspecting it with his claw. With one slight touch, the wood groaned, teetered, and fell to the ground, startling the crab, who took cover between big lakeside stones.

The shockwave from the pole snapped the rope that held the barrels to the vessel, sending a lone drum rolling away. From the outcrop of rocks, the crab panicked, seeing the barrel headed his way, and darted back into a crevasse of a boulder. The barrel rolled towards the crab's hiding spot at a crawl and nudged up to the rocks with a gentle tap. The crab emerged from his hiding place with careful, delicate steps and scaled the barrel, raising his claws in conquest.

Bort felt like he could be mad, but his face contorted into disappointment. For almost an entire year, Bort had devoted himself to building Hot Dog. Watching the mast collapse brought forth memories of when Bort had painstakingly hauled it back to his house from the market, held up the bus schedule strapping it to the snail, and taking an hour dragging it through the soft, sandy shores of Lake Lemnear.

The barrel that now rested by the rocks reminded Bort of the courage it had taken to ask the ale makers for a few empty Riverberry Ale barrels, which were hard to come by. Getting them to Lake Lemnear was a difficult task in itself. Bort had first had to learn to balance on top of them and walk each of them to the beach, since they were too big for him to push and could have gotten away from him with ease.

All his efforts were ruined in mere moments. Hot Dog's maiden voyage was an utter failure.

His thoughts and emotions spiraled. Bort wanted to cry, or scream, or laugh. His feelings were overwhelming. What was he supposed to do? Who was he going to blame? Should he just give up? It had taken so much time and effort to get as far as he had, and to think he would need to start all over again... Bort felt a bubbling fire fill his body and—

"Bort!" Bort yelled, squeezing his eyes shut as he punched and kicked the ground in a fit of fury.

After his outburst, Bort sat up, covered in sand, and folded his arms with a harsh and angry glare. He took a sharp breath and sighed with a curse. His tantrum relieved a bit of the pressure, giving him a second to think. Now he just felt stupid and humiliated.

Bort knew well within himself that he needed to calm down and take a deep breath; at least that's what others had told him to do in times like these. But how could anyone just breathe it out? It didn't make any sense! Such hollow words. There had to be a step missing. How could it be so easy as to shrug something off that made him feel so much? He felt even more pathetic as his emotions welled up with memories of past failures, he should "breathe out." More like swallow down and make your tummy hurt!

Like when he'd worked on new dishes for his pancake shop, which had failed, or when he'd burnt a new kind of pancake, or made what was supposed to be sweet syrup, sour. He would feel so upset and disheartened at himself. Bort would then heed the wisdom to breathe, move on, let go, and cheer up. But Bort only ever felt like it molded a mask around his face that smiled to the outside world, while within, it ate him to his core. It felt like he gulped a red-hot stone each and every time he tried. Failing at making the dish was only the catalyst for spurring the rapid onset of the emotional roller coaster. That single experience would drag his mind, heart, and spirit through the turmoil he faced within himself that would make him feel physically ill.

Bort was at least aware enough to see that he was only going in circles. In his peripheral, he saw a certain skreigull bird he'd been noticing since coming to the lake to design Hot Dog fly down and land on the now-broken mast. This skreigull was different than the other birds. It had the same multicolored, patterned feathers announcing it to be male. However, its pattern was rough and scattered. Not with any of the lustrous blues, greens, and yellows that its counterparts had. Their usual sleek and short tail feathers came to a point, but this one looked more like a cotton ball. His eyes never quite looked in the same direction, and his gait was more of a controlled stumble than a graceful step. He was, for lack of a better term, a dumpy skreigull, which he nicknamed Doughnut. Bort felt they were a well-suited pair.

Doughnut first came around when Bort would be staring off into the Spiral Cliffs, daydreaming of the Glimmering Sparrow and high adventures. They would watch one another for a while before moving on with their own plans; Bort to his drawings, Doughnut to his hunting. Skreigull birds often browsed the sands or shallow waters to eat small mollusks, but their favorite delicacy comprised of small minnows that were exceptionally difficult to catch.

As per usual, the two watched one another in their affectionate, yet awkward greeting. They both studied each other, tilting their heads. Satisfied with their formalities, Doughnut hopped off the broken ship to fish in the shallow waters. Doughnut bobbed up and down from the waves in the lake and fixated on the small fish swimming beneath him. Doughnut would strike into the water, attempting to catch the minnows but failed each time. Before long, he started thrashing and flapping around, growing frustrated as the minnows swam circles around him. In a last-ditch effort, Doughnut dove into the water and rolled onto his back as he remained buoyant. His feet kicked into the air, and he flapped his wings, trying to right himself. He was soon carried over to the shore, where the water spat him out and cartwheeled him along the sand, feet over beak.

Soaking wet, covered in sand, and panting, Doughnut waddled up next to Bort and plopped down on his rump for a break. His feet stuck out to his sides rather than underneath him, and he wore the same frustrated look as Bort.

Bort's eyes darted over in Doughnut's direction. Bort relaxed his tense shoulders, and his mind settled as he thought about Doughnut. Not once did Bort ever see Doughnut eat any mollusks, but only ever saw him spend the day fishing for fresh minnows. How long had he been hunting minnows even before Bort had started coming to the lake?

Bort's stomach rumbled. He looked at his belly, uncrossed his arms, waddled over to grab his morning snack from his pack, and sat back down with Doughnut. Bort pulled out a few pear-rots and took a bite of the delicious fruit. He then tore a smaller piece out with his mouth and tossed it over to Doughnut. Bort never liked to see anyone go hungry, so he'd made it a habit long ago to prepare enough for his little friend, who cocked his head and devoured his share. Bort would then take a bite of his own and lob another piece to Doughnut.

Satisfied with his rest and the snack Bort had provided, Doughnut was determined to return to his hunt and ended his break early. Bort chewed his last bite, watching Doughnut walk into the water. Not wanting the rest of Doughnut's share to go to waste, he took a series of tiny bites and tossed them in his direction. A few bits landed on the shore, as others tumbled into the lake where they floated. As the pear-rot bits bobbed in the lake, a school of minnows churned the water's surface as they consumed the piece of drifting fruit with blazing fervor. Doughnut shrieked in surprise and cocked his head, studying the minnows, then looked at the few bits on the beach and back to the fish. Doughnut hurried over to a floating pear-rot chunk, snatched it up, placed it in the water, and waited as still as a statue. Just like before, the minnows swam to the surface and devoured the fruit. Doughnut squawked in excitement before putting another piece in the water. Again, the minnows came up to devour the morsel. This time, Doughnut snatched a minnow and made haste for the shore.

Bort looked on in disbelief. After all this time, Doughnut caught one at last! Bort had no words. The earlier feelings of his failure were now a distant memory. Bort could not feel any shred of sadness; his mind was focused on the countless times Doughnut had failed in the past and how the hapless skreigull let his emotions flow through him. Doughnut would cry, squawk, throw tantrums, lie in the sand outright defeated, sulk, and sit next to Bort numb and catatonic. Yet, after the feelings had come and gone, Doughnut pulled himself together and got right back to fishing. Doughnut didn't waste time feeling sorry for himself, nor would he sit there and overthink anything like Bort did. He just let himself feel and process his emotions before getting right back to it. And here, finally, after so long, Doughnut's efforts had paid off.

Bort understood the lesson as clear as cellophane noodles. This was only his first attempt at building a boat. He came into it not even knowing a thing about building, and even less about captaining a ship. The little skreigull had failed countless times at the same task; how could Bort think he would ace it on the first try? Here was an excellent opportunity to learn. Bort learned how not to build a boat, how his craftsmanship could use some work — well, a lot of work — and, the most important, how much his feelings impacted him and could impede his progress. Bort's perspective on the situation had flipped head over tush, and the swirling despair of his emotions erupted into a spire of motivation.

Once Bort rose above his ocean of emotions, the lessons came one after the other without a break. First, Bort realized that failure was but part of the long, arduous road that was success. There might be many, many attempts needed before Bort would even come close to actualizing his dream, and the failures to learn might require a lot of time, work, and energy.

Another lesson learned was to be determined without giving up. Like Doughnut, he could not dwell on the failures. What would be the next step then? What was something Bort could try next time? What seemed to have worked in the failed attempt versus what hadn't? How could he use that opportunity to learn and be better? What good could come from something that many would consider a disaster?

Bort also began to understand the influential role of emotions, his thoughts, and how they could turn him into their puppet. Being consumed by feelings would make Bort act out on them and shut off from listening to anything helpful from the outside or from his own heart, filtering everything he was experiencing through whichever emotion restricted him at that moment. Like Doughnut, it was okay to feel and allow them to take their course, but never to pause on them for long.

Bort took the time to observe himself and felt the familiar spark of resolve. He knew he had to get back up and start again. But the feelings within him stagnated on his failure. The thought of all the hard work he'd put into Hot Dog was so daunting! Logically, Bort knew he had to continue, but he needed to let these feelings out. But how? Bort thought and thought, searching deep inside his guts for the answers as questions filled his little brain.

Bort closed his eyes and took a deep breath. He was used to this feeling from battling his amnesia. Anytime he was close to finding some answer or recalling a faint memory, usually a dozen new questions muddled his mind. Every new discovery begot even more questions, it seemed. Although it was as great to learn new things as it was to remember the fragments of his past, it always drained vast amounts of energy for Bort and triggered his phantom pain. But, he figured, if he wanted to be an adventurer like Lemnear, then more of himself would be required to be the Bort he aspires to be. The Bort that was today must chase the Bort that would be tomorrow and outpace the Bort that was yesterday. Failure was the pathway to success. Tomorrow would be a new day to try again. Like Hot Dog, he may not get it today, but if he kept at it, ultimately, he would find the answer sooner than never. All that required work and determination; loads of it.

Bort felt mad, but this time it wasn't the swirly, yucky kind of mad. This anger he felt was like a pure, clean-burning fire deep in his belly. He rose to his feet, balling his flippers, and screamed out to the lake, "Bort!" The anger reinvigorated him with the strength of mind to continue with his quest to become an adventurer, and his heart filled with determination. While Bort processed his thoughts, the swell of emotions within him depressurized, and he felt much lighter.

Bort grew earnest, his mind focused, and his spirit tempered. Bort could not give up now! If he had to build the boat for the rest of his days to achieve his dream of becoming an adventurer, then so be it! His resolution would not be wiped out without a fight. Bort retrieved his flag, rolling it up, and headed for the bus stop. He paused to take one last look back at Hot Dog, the lake, and Doughnut, who was now catching more minnows, promising to return with a new plan.

It was at that moment that inspiration hit him: "Bo(You may not get the things you dream of, but you will always get the things you work for.)rt," Bort said to himself.

Bort smiled and nodded. How familiar, he thought just as a rush of phantom pain coursed in his head. Bort winced and held his head until it passed. That was strange, but no matter. Bort felt good with the lessons he'd learned and happy that he did not feel so glum from his failure anymore. Before heading back through the docks and shops, he looked back into the sky. With a renewed perspective, the day shined with endless possibilities. The clouds, the planets, the Skylands; all were magnificent and swelled his heart with joy.

54

CHAPTER XI

Wholesome Pancakes

Ding!

The bell chimed, announcing the bus's departure. The giant snail slithered onward, towards its next scheduled stop, leaving a bite-sized Bort waving thanks and fair-winds at Watertail Plaza. Bort found his morning walks from the bus stop to his house very peaceful and meditative. At this time of the morning, the sun beamed through the thick canopy overhead, lighting up the mountain-forest floor with rays of light and painted Lemnear in hues of green. A hush still lingered over the town, save for the devoted morning martial-art and fitness practitioners grinding through their routines, perfecting their crafts. While the erhu and flute players harmonized with the songs of nature, and bread makers filled the crisp mountain air with tantalizing aromas that wafted through the town. During his commute, Bort had no real thoughts and simply enjoyed being, and every now and again, waving good morrow to a fellow passerby.

Arriving home, Bort found his morning regulars, who were accustomed to his early morning lake visits, awaiting his return. His most frequent patron was Gar, the ancient Kura-Kura who'd resided in Lemnear longer than anyone could remember; an elderly tortoise with big bushy eyebrows over his slanted eyes, with a mustache and long, straight beard that all but touched the forest floor. His hair was tied up atop his head and plumed out like a straw broom. He hailed from unheard-of isles far from Lemnear that are allegedly located off the southeast corner of the continent of Meliae. Gar still donned the traditional robes of his island. In all his long-lived years, Gar had never tasted anything as good as Bort's pancakes and fell in love with them at first bite. Gar seldom spoke without jokes or fables that were out of this world, rendering it difficult to discern if the incredible stories he spun were true, or the ramblings of an old man. Regardless, he was well liked by the children of Lemnear and, of course, Bort.

Bort walked up to Gar, who waited for the shop to open at the bottom of the steps. "Bort!" Bort greeted with a dulcet tone.

Gar turned to face Bort, aided by his cane, which somehow looked older than him. He shuffled towards Bort at a deliberate pace with a pleased mumble and gave a slight bow of his head, returning the greeting through his elderly tremors. "Back from the lake so soon, are we now, Bart?" Gar said, adjusting his cane.

Gar had been coming to eat habitually every day since Bort opened his shop, but getting his name right still eluded him. "Bo(It's Bort.)rt," Bort corrected him yet again, as if it was the first time Gar got it wrong. "Bo(And, yeah, it looks like I still have my work cut out for me)rt," Bort said, embarrassed.

"Bah!" Gar said and made a gesture with his gnarled hand, scoffing at the idea of having to put more work into Bort's dream. "Anything easy is not worth it, boy-o, and anything worth it is not easy," Gar said in a kind and uplifting manner.

Whether or not the old man was spouting sweet, elderly expressions or not, his words lifted Bort's heart. "There is nothing more important than working to achieve your dreams, lad! Otherwise, you would only be wishing, and nothing can happen on wishes alone. So, work, Billy! Work until your dream fits easily within your grasp, and then dream some more! Ha-ha-ha!" the old tortoise laughed.

Bort smiled and stepped beside Gar to assist him up the stairs and into the restaurant. "Bo(It's Bort)rt," he said once more, "Bo(and you're right! I will keep working, so I can dream more with all of my whole heart!)rt!"

"That's my boy! Now, how about some of those delicious pancakes while you lead your dreams, Bert?" Gar said, excited for his pancakes.

"Bort," Bort corrected. "Bo(The usual wolfberry cream double-stack with berry-jam compote?)rt?"

"That's my lad," Gar said, patting Bort's hand as they made their way up the stairs.

Halfway up the steps, Bort's second familiar face awaited him, a well-shaped petite Ulgan named Neona. The Ulgan peoples were more akin to avians and primarily nocturnal by nature. Thus, it was commonplace for many of them to do overnight jobs such as at inns, bars, guard posts, and maintenance facilities. They had a strong affinity for music, so many in Lemnear followed their hearts and became bards and dancers. Neona was no exception. She ran the Moonless Light Tavern, where she offered weary travelers and locals rooms and meals and entertained them with song and dance. In dim lighting, her large crystalline, iridescent eyes eerily mirrored the colors of the moon, but in the daytime, they reflected lovely metallic silver. Her feathers were mostly red with streaks of white, while her chest was solid white feathers save for a few pattern reds. She donned elegant belts, flowing skirts, and wispy blouses; typical bard garb. For her, her meal at this time of day would be dinner.

Neona smiled and curtseyed her unique bards greeting: "Good morrow to you, my child," she said with seductive elegance and class, never ceasing from being a hostess herself.

"Bo(Good Morning — err — night, Neona!)rt," Bort said.

She giggled before speaking once more. "Have you found your dreams yet?"

Bort sighed, closed his eyes, and shook his head. "Bo(Mnh, nope... But I won't give up.)rt," he said.

"Atta boy, Barnacles!" Gar said.

"It's Bort," Bort said in a pleasant voice, correcting him again with a smile.

Neona brought her hands together. "That's the spirit, my child," she said and spun in a circle with poise, producing a bodhran. "If you will, allow me to enchant a song of rejuvenation and fortune for you this morning," she said, beating her drum.

"Bo(I would love that! Yay! Music!!)rt!" Bort said and hopped with anticipation, bouncing Gar along with him. Neona smiled and began slow twirls, playing her bodhran as she hummed, excited to be able to perform once more before her dinner.

Bort continued to the door, where his most peculiar patron waited as patiently as he could at the top of the stairs. A Laskan named — well, no one really knew, but he answered to Bomber.

Laskans resembled weasels and originated from across the Luagal Sea. He was long and lanky with stubby arms and legs. His underbelly was covered with yellow fur, while his back was brown. He preferred walking on all fours but spent half his time bipedal. He dressed in unmatched armor that he'd pieced together haphazardly, adding more to it each time he found something he liked at the market. Bomber worked as a guardsman at the East tower during the graveyard shift. His title and position were anyone's guess.

Bort made his way to the entrance. Bomber swayed his body like a pendulum, awaiting Bort. Bomber began rubbing his hands together and hopped on his feet. "Hi-hi-hi-hi! Hee, hee!" Bomber said in his usual bizarre manner, which Bort found endearing. "Bort," Bort said in kind with a wave of his flipper.

Bomber dropped to all fours and faced the door, bounding in place while Bort unlocked the restaurant. Gar shuffled in, mumbling to himself first and then moved to the side as Neona played her drum, sang, and twirled in. Bomber stood back up and lumbered in, stopping only to grab Bort's flipper, shaking it a few times in thanks.

"Bo(The usual bacon waffles and pancakes topped with stinky cheese?)rt?" Bort asked, having memorized the strange order the first time he'd made it, because that was one of Bort's failed wonders, which he must've left out, and it had found its way into Bomber's stomach.

"Yah-yah-yah-yah! Stinky cheese! Hah-hah! Bacon! Hmm, hmm!" Bomber said, letting go of Bort's flipper. He clapped to himself and licked his chops. "Ahh Hee, hee!," Bomber said, making his way to his favorite seat at the counter while whistling.

Bort smiled. He enjoyed his group of oddball regulars that made mornings fun and exciting. They were so much a part of the restaurant that Bort couldn't imagine them not being there. They had developed such a relationship that it was not uncommon for them to bring Bort gifts, and vice versa.

Bort loved cooking meals that brought so many different people together and made for so many great memories. He held birthdays, events, celebrations,

and parties at his restaurant. Anything that served to fill his kitchen with love, laughter, and joy. Even if they were bittersweet times. Since Bort struggled so much with amnesia, making fond memories that he could hold on to meant everything to him. Unknown to anyone, he drew pictures of the events, stories, and people he had met and did his best to write them down in his Great Big Book of Remembories.

Cooking seemed to be the only thing that bridged the gap over his amnesia and made him feel right with whatever was before Lemnear. It was also comforting to him, because it was the only way he felt capable of helping anyone. For him, although it was a small task, filling hungry tummies was an important one, and one he knew he could do with his whole heart. The restaurant crammed with villagers, and Bort went about his day filling orders, making meals, and cleaning up. Before long, the restaurant laid empty, and Bort was on his last task, mopping the dining floor.

Bort had two times a day where he was the busiest: mornings and early dinner time. In between those hours, the restaurant was closed, allowing Bort to take his trusty wooden wagon into the market to pick the freshest ingredients and to flipper-pick the dinner, the Pancake Supreme Chef's Special Ultra Turbo Edition he custom made each day.

As his dishes became more and more popular, many of the market vendors approached Bort and pleaded for him to use their products in his meals. In turn, the vendors gained notoriety for their superb ingredients and thus would be ranked higher in their crafts. Bort loved the challenge of creating new fusion flavors, presenting his food like art pieces and, of course, being able to eat all the unique ingredients he could get his grubby flippers on. Some of his chef's-special dishes were so good, they would make the village headlines; other times, Bort ended up stuck in the bathroom all night with dinner hours sometimes being cancelled.

CHAPTER XII

Super Not-So-Secret Secret Adventure-Hero Training!

After Bort finished midday errands for the dinner rush, he began his super-not-so-secret secret adventure-hero training! If he were going to be an adventurer and scale the Spiral Cliffs, he would need to be courageous, strong, and witty just like Lemnear! Bort tied a bandana around his head and brought his clenched fists to his sides, his eyes teeming with purpose. The fire in his belly blazed as he placed one flipper on the picture of Lemnear before bolting out the door to begin his session.

In his mind, the whole world turned into a video game where Bort would gain experience points based on how well he trained. Bort's exercises consisted of everything he thought were the most important, like calisthenics! Jumping! Belly sliding! Eating! Balancing! Mental strength! Checkers! And the most perilous of all: sneaky egg pinching! The last on the list also served to acquire ingredients, so this was like a boss fight in Bort's head.

Bort took in a slow deep breath as he stood at the entrance of the chicken coop. No matter how brave he tried to be, the chickens terrified him down to his very core. Their pecks were accurate, their talons sharp, and the speed they struck with was horrifying. While Bort's spirit burned bright, and his heart tempered with resolve, his body trembled in fear. But not even the sound of his boney knees rattling together would keep him from trying for the three hundredth time. In his many attempts, Bort had constructed different strategies to snatch the eggs, from dressing up as a chicken, to sneaking in like a ninja, to pretending to be a chick; each had their strengths and weaknesses.

However, Bort's best strategy was donning a thick cotton-armor suit equipped with a shield, basket, and helmet that Garlic had helped him sew together. It was good defense and provided Bort with a sense of security. Besides, it made him feel really cool like a knight, a courageous pancake knight. Bort's helmet was topped with a chicken feather that he alone plucked from one of the mighty chickens. Bort wore it with pride as a testament to his bravery, even though he ran out the coop screaming both in terror and delight, holding his bounty overhead.

Bort put his game face on and got into his gear while running through the day's tactics in his mind. He decided to spend less time on the gentler hens, who

laid plain eggs, and go for the stronger, more aggressive ones. They had the prettiest eggs and tested his merit. There were five all together. He'd named each by their temperament and combative skills.

There was Big Red. She was big and strong, but easy to dodge. Her eggs were large and teal in color. Hers were best for batters and omelets.

Grumpelstilsken had the meanest and quickest pecks. She flapped about a lot, and her squawks were paralyzing. But the gorgeous blue eggs she laid always had golden yolks. These were best for sunny-side-up eggs for breakfasts and soups.

Sergeant Shiny Sides was the hardest to outrun. She was swift, with lightning-fast reflexes. She scarcely ever pecked, but she'd fluffed up and trampled over Bort many times with her sharp talons. Her eggs, which she laid by the dozens, were small and deep green. These eggs were best boiled.

Finally, there was Mr. Fluffy Feets. To Bort, she was the main boss, the head honcho, the top cluck. She was the biggest and hardest to get away from. Her power was not in her beak or her claws — oh, no — but through her googly, cross-eyed gaze, which struck terror deep into Bort's heart. It was the face of a strong maternal instinct. She regularly mistook Bort's fluffy cotton-armor for one of her chicks and would pluck him up and enshrine him with love and care. He had failed every time he'd tried for one of her eggs and spent the remainder of the day stuck under her loving bosom. Her eggs were big, beautiful, and spattered with intricate designs. It was her eggs Bort sought most of all.

Bort took a deep breath and swallowed hard. Mr. Fluffy Feets had a secret weapon that shook Bort's resolve even at the thought of it. Once, long ago, Bort had been able to get his flippers on one of her eggs. When her pea-sized brain had realized he wasn't one of hers, she fluffed up and shot her head to the sky with a bellowing war-cluck. The entire coop hushed as the ground shook, and from the nesting boxes, it came. Bort dared not utter his name aloud, but he called him Doodle-Doo, because that was the sound the rooster had made before Bort was struck unconscious, waking up in the apothecary. The few times he'd seen Doodle-Doo, the bird had been big, mean, and with battle-worn feathers, and he'd struck with ire.

Bort shut his eyes and shook Doodle-Doo from his mind, trying not to lose his grit. With mitted flippers, he unlatched the gate and once again, stepped knee-deep into the fowl fray. Bort searched the pockets of his suit and procured a map of the coop and his many hiding spots. With a grunt and a nod, Bort put his map away and placed his helmet over his head. Today would be the day, the day he did not fall to the might and prowess of the hens!

The gate to the coop shut behind him. He had his pillow-shield at the ready and his woven basket in hand. Shaking, he descended deeper into the nightmare.

Still afraid of getting pecked, he snatched a few eggs from the more docile chickens like an adept thief. Anytime he woke a hen by mistake, he ran away in a silent, panic-stricken manner and made use of his hidey-holes. Once the coast was clear, Bort mustered his courage and continued his mission.

Sometime later, Bort looked at the bounty in his basket, satisfied, as it brimmed with each kind of rare egg. He was able to dodge around Big Red, cover his ears from

Grumpelstilsken's paralyzing screech, and used his shield against Sergeant Shiny Sides' blitzes. Bort had not been this successful ever! With high spirits, it was then he decided to go up against the final boss, Mr. Fluffy Feets.

By the grace of the pancakes, she was fast asleep, and Bort slithered next to her, unobstructed. His flippers shook with such anticipation, that he had to take a second to calm his nerves. Each egg was beautiful, ornately speckled with designs, and felt like unblemished porcelain. Not wanting to get greedy, Bort only took a few, careful not to wake her. "Bo(Phew.)rt," Bort said, and wiped his brow. He glided back away from her like a phantom, keeping his eyes trained on her, not noticing Grumpelstilsken scratching at the ground behind him. As he turned to leave the coop, his basket bumped Grumpelstilsken, causing her to cackle, flap her wings, and run off. Bort calcified in terror as he watched her dash around the chicken run before the dreaded sounds of Mr. Fluffy Feets waking clucks drained all color from Bort's face. Her shadow soon loomed over him as he turned towards her and stared into the heart-shaped, cross-eyed glare of maternal doom.

"Bort!"

Bort spun around, running away as fast as he could to his nearest hidey-hole, all the while screaming and flailing his flippers high into the sky, throwing his shield and basket through the air in a panic. Before Bort could even get more than a few steps away, Mr. Fluffy Feets bounded towards him, closing the distance in an instant. She plucked him up by the feather in his helmet while Bort, with one final Borty wail, was snatched up and placed into her nest. It all happened so fast that before he knew it, he was engulfed into the cozy soft darkness of Mr. Fluffy Feets' bosom.

Game Over.

Mr. Fluffy Feets nestled with masterful care on top of Bort as he fought to get away, popping out his head, then a flipper, a leg, and finally a butt from underneath her, trying with maximum effort to escape. But she stuffed him back under her with her beak without much struggle. If he were able to break free, Bort would run as fast as his little legs could take him, making do with whatever eggs he'd be able to recover in the process. But unable to escape, he needed to wait until she fell back asleep. Once her breathing became rhythmic, Bort emerged from Mr. Fluffy Feets' feathers and made his break for it. Retrieving his shield and basket of whatever eggs remained, Bort flew through the gate, shutting it behind him, and didn't look back.

CHAPTER XIII

The Junior Ensign Ironmight Knights!

Bort plodded along the cobblestone pathway with a sour face. Defeat sure didn't taste good anymore. The wagon carried his armor and basket of eggs, squeaking in sync with his steps. He was able to recover less than half of his bounty; the rare eggs left behind, smashed. However, still, hanging onto the lesson of failure being a step towards success, he wasted no time wallowing in defeat. It only strengthened his desire to try again. Bort huffed as his mind went over his egg-raid tactics and what he could do differently next time.

From off in the distance, the sounds of children laughing and clashing sticks echoed through the town. Three Popoki siblings were playing off the path to Bort's house. The Popoki people were closely related to Wildings and resemble felines. Although they were one race, they, like the Ulgans, fell into different subspecies. Therefore, their looks and physiques could differ dramatically.

Bort's familiar-sounding squeaky wagon caught the attention of a girl in her teens, Castor. She sparred with the only boy in the group, who was her fraternal twin. Her eyes were dark blue, sleek, and large, accentuated by natural eyeliner. Castor's crimson hair was short, spiky, and framed her face. But behind her, it was tamed in a ponytail that ran the length of her back. She wore her school uniform, a short pleated blue skirt and a midriff blue, white, and red top. She donned a stick as a sword, a trashcan lid for a shield, and a pot for a helmet.

Her brother, Pollux, had straight, layered, chocolate-colored, chin-length hair and heterochromatic eyes. One was dark blue, and the other a cherry red. He wore blue athletic shorts with a blue, red, and white school-team shirt. Pollux had tied his school jacket around his shoulders to use as a cape and held an old broom handle as a staff. After their sticks clashed, she kicked him away and sent him to the ground before her ears twitched, picking up the sound of Bort's wagon.

Before Castor could look in Bort's direction, the youngest sibling, Roisin, who'd turned nine last month, hugged tightly onto a Bort plushy. She wore a solid navy-blue pleated skirt and top, with an oversized bomber jacket that her hands didn't quite fit through. Her face lit up, and she bounded in place, pointing. "Hey, look ev'we one! It's Bwort! It's Bwort!" she exclaimed, her long, flowing, brown hair kept in place by oversized goggles atop her head. Her cherry-red eyes, too big for her head, resembled gumdrops as they sparkled. Pollux sat up from the ground, holding his head, until he heard Bort's name and looked up in excitement.

Castor smiled and wiped her nose with her arm as she hollered, "Hey, sensei," waving in the air, running towards Bort with the others tailing behind.

Bort, lost in his thoughts, didn't hear the children right away. He was preoccupied, working through an elaborate strategy on snatching the biggest bounty of rare eggs for tomorrow. It involved a bucket of ice, a ball of yarn, and a pogo stick. After a while, Bort's ears twitched as the racket the kids were making brought him from his scheming. In an instant, the plan he concocted retreated into the vault of his ideas, where it was shelved next to his plan to scare a tree and see if it would petrify. Noticing the three Popoki children running his way perked up his spirit.

Bort met the siblings soon after discovering the book, Raehern Erohan Vesstan's Wonderous Collections of Myths, Might, and Magic, Volume One In Garlic's library, where he was read the tale of Lemnear Risai T'Leia. It was then that he decided to follow the path to become an adventurer and began his super-secret training.

LAST SPRING

"Bor--t!" Bort growled between great strains of breath, trying to touch his feet. He had tied a rope around his ankles, thrown it over a branch, tied the other end to a heavy rock, and tossed it. The rock had pulled Bort up and suspended him in mid-air. Earlier that day, he watched one of Garlic's martial-arts movies, the Jade Dagger. Bort had been so inspired by the training montage that he had to try suspended sit ups.

It was then that while the three Popoki siblings played in the Lemnear forest that they found Bort dangling out of the tree. Bort then found himself surrounded by the trio, who wondered what he was doing.

"Hey, mister! Haven't seen you around before. What'cha doin'?" Castor said and walked up to Bort.

Bort opened his eyes and let his flippers hang down and spun, accompanied by the sound of groaning rope. "Bo(Hello…)rt…" Bort said, and waited to complete his rotation. "Bo(…upside down…)rt…" He paused. "Bo(…girl!)rt!" he said, smiled, and began to struggle for his feet once more, now twirling in the air.

"Bo(I'm… doing… secret… hero…adventure… training…)rt!" he said amid grunts, strains, and spins.

"Hey, you talk funny, mister," Pollux said as he walked up to Castor, studying Bort.

Roisin then walked up to him with a finger in her mouth, and her face flushed red. She was enamored with the way Bort looked. He appeared exactly like the stuffed animals she loved so much. She lowered her head with her eyes trained on Bort and dropped her clasped hands in front of her, "I'm Roisin, wuts your name, mister?" she said, fidgeting.

Bort relaxed, dangling from the tree with his flippers overhead, waiting to speak as he spun back around to face the children. "Bo(Nice to meet you, Roisin. Wanna train with me?)rt?" he said before spinning back around.

Roisin's face turned a brighter shade of red, and hid behind Castor. "Ha-ha! I think she likes you," Castor said. Roisin punched Castor's leg before clutching tighter on the hem of Castor's skirt and frowned.

"I'm Castor," the teen girl said, pointing a thumb at herself before nodding in the direction of Pollux. "And this is my bro, Pollux."

"Yo!" Pollux said and held a hand up in greeting.

Bort brought his flipper to his face, struck a pose, and returned the greeting with a musical, "Bort," while spinning.

"N', of course, this here's our kid sister, Roisin," Castor said. "Together we are the Junior Ensign Ironmight Knights of the Lemnear guard! We make sure everything is doin' a-oh-kay here in Lemnear! It's a really important job, you know?" Castor said, crossing her arms and holding her head up high.

"Bo(Oooh... You guys do a great job! Nice to meet the Ironmight Knights!)rt," Bort said, no longer pausing between spins. "Bo(I am Bort. And I am in the middle of my super-not-so-secret secret adventure-hero training! I wanna become an adventurer just like Lemnear!)rt!" he said.

"Eh, don't take her so seriously," Pollux said as he put his arms behind his head. "We're not really part of the Lemnear guard."

If looks could kill, Pollux would have been vaporized. Castor shot her hands to her sides, glowering at Pollux. "Shut up! Once they notice how hard we work, we'll be in the academy in no time flat!" she said, closing her eyes, took a deep breath, and folded her arms. "Just you wait. You'll see!" she added and snickered.

Pollux looked off with disdain and spat. "Tch! We aren't even a real group they'll recognize anyway," he said as a deep pain washed over his face; being a part of the knights' guard is all he ever dreamed about.

Roisin's face filled with sorrow. It seemed she shared the dream of being in the academy along with her brother and sister. Bort observed their faces and spoke from his heart. "Bo(I think what is most important is that you guys do your duty because it fulfills your heart of hearts! No matter what! Even if the Knights' guard can't see how amazing you all are, you should do what feels right for yourselves. I think that they won't have any other choice but to see how hard you guys work and will have to accept the Junior Ensign Ironmight Knights into the

academy!)rt!"

Bort's words cheered the children up. "Hey… Yeah, you're right," Pollux said.

"We should give it everything we've got!" Castor said.

"Yeah!" the trio shouted in unison, reinvigorated.

"Bo(Yeah!)rt!" Bort yelled with determination and worked to reach his toes with more gusto.

The kids watched Bort with his renewed fire. "Hey! I got a great idea! Why don't we train with Bort? You can be like our sensei!" Castor said, inspired. Caught off guard by her own enthusiasm, she tried playing it cool. "Erm, you know… cuz the Ironmights can help you, too, ya see…. L-like a trade," she blathered.

"Yeah! I wanna! I wanna!" Roisin gasped before she cried out in excitement, jumping at Castor's skirt.

"Yeah! That's a great idea," Pollux said and dropped to the ground for push-ups.

The four underwent their first training routine. Each struggled and strained, pushing themselves to their limits. It was here that the Junior Ensign Ironmight Knights fell under the tutelage of the aspiring hero-adventurer, Bort. Time passed, and it was not long before the Ironmight Knights lay on the ground, exhausted.

Bort struggled one last time to reach his toes before falling slack. His flippers dangled towards the ground as he caught his breath.

"Bo(Boy! This sure is great that you guys decided to train with me,)rt," Bort said.

"Yeah! I didn't realize it was going to be so tough," Castor said in between breaths.

"Bo(It sure is! Just ending training is really hard. I stopped my super-not-so-secret secret adventure-hero training about twenty minutes ago!)rt!" Bort said, high spirited.

"Huh? You stopped? The whole time I was trying to keep up with you! And I was even taking breaks," Castor said, surprised.

Bort's big brown eyes looked her way. "Bo(Oh, that was me just trying to get my feet out of the rope… I'm stuck,)rt," he said, not having the forethought to figure out how he would get down.

"Oh! Dis sownds like a jowb for dah Junior Enthign Irownmight Knights!" Roisin said.

The Ironmight Knights tried to get to their feet, but to no avail.

"We will help… once we catch our breath," Pollux said, sticking a finger in the air.

"Y-yeah… J-just give us a minute," Castor said.

Powerless, Bort dangled in the air, spinning in circles as they caught their breath. Less concerned with his predicament, he was more thrilled to have fellow training partners. He stretched his flippers with a great big smile on his face. "Bo(Adventure training!)rt!" he shouted.

"Yeah," The children said, exhausted, each raising an arm to the air.

PRESENT

"Bo(Hello!)rt!" Bort said.

"He-ya, sensei! How ya doin'?" Castor said.

Bort growled with a stinky face.

"The adventure training didn't go well today, eh, sensei?" Pollux asked.

"Bo(Argh… I was defeated again… By Mr. Fluffy Feets.)rt." Bort huffed. Realizing his training was subpar, he turned his gaze to the sky and felt the breeze on his face. His eyes brimmed with purpose. "Bo(I need to train harder!)rt!" Bort said and balled his fist.

Roisin raced up to Bort and jumped around him in a circle. "It's okay! We still have a lowt of twraining to do to," she said, comforting him.

"Thensei! Thensei!" Roisin said, grabbing Bort's flipper, and bounced up and down. "Will you take us wif you to see your boat, thensei? We pwomise to catch you a lot of shuggie slugs if you do," she pleaded.

Hot Dog! Bort was so engrossed in his training that he'd forgotten all about his boat sinking! Bort paused and slapped a flipper to his forehead.

"Bo(ugh!)rt…" Bort groaned. He pulled down at his face, keeping his eyes trained to the sky. So much to do! Bort needed to up his training and start all over on Hot Dog. He began walking again, grumbled, and explained the morning events to his students, from riding his bucket coaster down from his treehouse, to the rope, the ship taking on water, diving into the lake to tug Hot Dog back to shore, the crab, and to Doughnut.

"Aww, that's the pits, sensei," Pollux said, drooping his ears.

"I'm sorry too, sensei," Castor said, walking next to Bort.

"That sownds scawy," Roisin said, hugging her stuffed Bort doll closer, burrowing her face into it.

Bort relaxed. Blurting out his frustrations helped him vent his feelings. He smiled, shaking his head. "Bo(It's okay, Roisin. I learned a lot from it.)rt," Bort said and raised his head to the sky. "Bo(Besides, I'm pretty good at swimming, ya know?)rt?" he added.

"Did you see any monsters or sharks in the water, sensei?" Castor said, showing a hint of fear of the creatures that might dwell in the bottom reaches of the lake.

"Bo(Nope, no monsters. Just skreigulls and minnows) rt," Bort said, looking to each kid as they ask their questions. "Bo(I did hope to hunt for some yummy slugs, though. But I couldn't catch any, because I was too busy trying to save Hot Dog.) rt," he said, scratching behind his head, humiliated.

"Hey, I know," Castor said. She ran ahead of Bort and twirled around to face him. "How about we all go next time and hunt for some slugs for you, sensei? Maybe that will brighten your spirits a bit. Maybe there'll be some treasure and stuff along the beach that you can use for your boat," she said.

"Bo(Hey! Yeah! That's a great idea.)rt," Bort said, excited.

"Yeah!" the kids said in unison.

"It's what the Ironmight Knights do best!" Castor exclaimed.

"I'm the best at finding slugs," Pollux said with a smirk on his face. "I'll cast a reveal spell and find all of them before anyone else," he said and pointed his stick to cast a spell.

Roisin's face crinkled as she placed her goggles over her eyes. "Nuh-uh! I will find all dem furst! Wif my super-speshual findy eyes," she said, running ahead with her arms up as if flying, the jacket sleeves flapping behind her as she ran and scoured the ground for slugs.

A broad grin grew on Castor's face. "Oh yeah? I think it will be no use against heart, determination, and the fire in my belly to never give up! You should quit now and save yourselves the agony!" Castor said, running with the Junior Ensign

Ironmight Knights on their quest for slugs.

The children zig-zagged through the forest, searching for any slugs, bugs, and beetles that may be about, making a competition out of it. Bort watched them run off and turn a corner before disappearing into the trees in the town.

The thought of being able to work on his boat, further his adventure training, all the while, enjoying life with friends around him, washed away the tough emotions he'd held on to. Bort would've been lying if he'd said he didn't feel excited to head down to the lake with the Junior Ensign Ironmight Knights. The refreshing wave of fervor cheered him up and motivated him to start his dreams all over again.

From the market plaza, Bort heard the clock bells announce the hour. It was just about time to head back to the restaurant and prepare the dinner menu. Moreover, at this time of day during summer, the sun shimmered impeccably onto the living bridge by his house.

The unique living bridges were used to cross the many rivers, streams, and falls that meandered throughout the town. Like the mighty sequoia trees, they were one of the marvels exclusive to Lemnear. These bridges were made up of tree roots that had been maintained for decades with great care. In fact, entire family lineages had dedicated themselves to tending to these bridges for generations. It was a great mystery when the people of Lemnear began making them, but the eldest bridge that connected the rest of Lemnear to Bort's Pancake Shop over the Bronwyn Falls was said to be as old as the town itself.

When Bort set out for the early mornings, the heavy mists of the falls obscured the breathtaking scenery of the bridge. Now at midday, the haze billowed up from the falls, bending sunbeams that filtered through the canopy, and painted a cloudy, dreamlike realm. The depth of browns and greens from the bridge accentuated the old pieces of blue-grey stone. Each of them had been handcrafted and laid across the bridge. Some of the rocks were engraved with characters from an ancient language long since forgotten. The sediment that collected around the bridge sprouted new life of glowing stargrass and sproutlings. Some branches were left to grow, creating the illusion of trees on the bridge. They were well-traveled and maintained daily. The stones on the floor of the bridge were level and smooth, never once being problematic for Bort to tug his wagon across.

Staring off into Bronwyn Falls, Bort was startled by the clock bells as they rang once more. Bort shook his head and pushed off the root that acted as the bridge's railing. Had he really daydreamed for so long? It felt like only a matter of moments had passed and not an entire hour. Even after living here for a year, he was still captivated by the magic and beauty of Lemnear. Bort grabbed the handle of his wagon and made his way back home with a renewed and calm heart.

CHAPTER XIV

Dissatisfaction

Bort filled his jars of herbs and spices with fresh ingredients from the market and arranged them within reach. He chopped vegetables, set his soup stocks to simmer, and made his secret batters in preparation for the dinner rush. Before long, Bort had his entire kitchen and restaurant ready before his three regulars strolled in, announced by Bomber's long neck poking through the windows of the foyer. The entry bells chimed as Bort opened the door with a welcoming smile. Excited to see Bort, Bomber chuckled as he shook his hand in greeting before he slinked back down the steps, assisting Gar into the pancake shop with Neona twirling in behind the two.

Today's Pancake Supreme Chef Special Ultra Turbo Edition started off with braised-mammoth soup to whet the appetite, followed by the main course, seafood vegetable-filled potato pancakes with eel dipping sauce and finished with a hearty helping of chocolate cream dragonturtle cobbler for dessert. Bort served and cooked for his friends, who'd come in with empty bellies, making sure they left fuller in their tummies as well as in their hearts. Bort's house soon packed with the warmth, music, light, and laughter of the townsfolk. Daylight waned, and the town darkened sooner before the last rays of sun beamed over the mountains from the thick canopy overhead, causing the colorful lights and signs of the village to come to life before twilight.

Bort loved cooking, especially when he could share it with friends, townsfolk and well, anyone who was interested in tasting his cuisine that he poured his whole soul into. But today, Bort caught himself sighing, unable to concentrate, and his thoughts wandered off. He found himself staring longer and longer into the painting of Lemnear; so long, in fact, that he forgot about the cauldron of braised-mammoth soup as it boiled over.

"Erm, my child, it is not my place to interfere with your master craft, but I believe..." Neona said and pointed a winged claw towards the clamoring pot of soup.

Bort followed her finger with his eyes and yelped, and rushed over to save the broth. There was no more doubt in his mind that something was bothering him to the point that it distracted him from cooking. Bort couldn't pinpoint it, but his heart panged with longing. Staring into Bronwyn Falls, Bort had reflected on his free time spent working on Hot Dog and super-not-so-secret secret adventure-hero training. Though it had been peppered with failure, the effort had felt more fulfilling than usual. From Hot Dog setting the world record for sinking ships, to the bitter taste of fluffy feet defeat, all of it burned pure; the lessons, valuable, and the inspiration to try harder set his spirit ablaze.

"Are you all right, my child? You seem distracted," Neona asked.

Bort placed a flipper behind his head and smiled. "Bo(Yeah, I think I had too much fun today training. I may have overdone it)rt," he said.

Neona relaxed in her seat and smiled. "Good, my child. Give it all that you've got," she said, "but be sure to pace yourself and not get overwhelmed. Commit each measure you take with all your heart, one step at a time."

"Bo(You bet!)rt!" Bort said, throwing his flippers in the air, thankful for her imparting wisdom.

Night soon came, and Bort's Pancake Shop laid empty save for Gar, who enjoyed helping Bort clean. Once finished, Bort thanked him with some take-home goodies, escorted him down the steps, and waived fair-winds to Gar as he shuffled off to his home to retire.

After Gar was out of sight, Bort walked back into his restaurant to finish the last few tasks. All was silent, save for the crickets, cicadas, and owls. Alone with his thoughts, the longing in his heart rolled like thunder, and his dissatisfaction spread like wildfire. With mop in hand, Bort gazed off into nothing. The feelings were disturbing and scary, like what he felt when sorting the mystery of his past. It felt like being in a room full of people but being unequivocally alone.

Mopping often helped Bort meditate and unwind. Which was, by and large, followed up by relaxing with some video games, going to Firefox Pub for Realms and Ravens night, gazing at the stars from Castle Bort, or meeting up with Xoey and Garlic for a movie. Tonight, the dissatisfaction that he felt was crushing. Unable to focus on his task, Bort hastened his pace to finish, fixated on his sense of urgency to put in the work to lead his dreams.

Bort felt compelled to act. Driven by his aching heart, he needed to do something. With a flipper caressing Lemnear's painting, Bort closed his kitchen and walked out the door. He grabbed his wagon from the side of the house, hoping a walk in the misty night air would clear his mind, and maybe he would find something, anything. The sound of squishy footfalls and a squeaky wagon echoed down the pathway towards the town center.

There was an hour left before most shops closed in the Secret Hollow Grove District. Festive music played in the hollowed tree as villagers partook in the nightlife. Warmth and light from pubs spilled into the street, emphasized by muffled laughter and clattering tankards. Fireflies wisped through the corridor, and minor wildings sauntered along, adding to the peaceful ambiance.

It was heartening to see the town so full of life and harmony. Throughout the seasons, Lemnear looked radically different, in particular, during the festivals and many holidays. It was normal for Bort to feel a sense of comfort from Lemnear's predictability, the convenience of getting anything he needed, along with amusing himself at the various shops and eateries. The villagers were generally pleasant and helpful, and the town was so stunning that many other townships paled in comparison to the fairy-tale beauty of Lemnear. Bort loved Lemnear and all she had to offer.

However, the uneasiness in Bort's heart eclipsed the town and exposed how boring it could be. It all felt the same to him. Tonight, the town only served as a reminder of his own predictable routine. It was extremely unsettling to realize that he'd droned away his days instead of leading each one with intention.

But as Bort thought about it more, it troubled him every night. It was the first time he was consciously aware of it. One whole year had passed since he'd come to Lemnear, and in those first few weeks, he'd tried relentlessly to remember anything from his past. But fulfilling his curiosity and wonder had begun to take priority. As time passed, Bort became more comfortable, finding a life to live in Lemnear, enjoying the friendships he had made, and becoming a loved member of the community.

Less and less, Bort focused inward, forgetting about what made him feel whole. It was a slow and gradual change that occurred without him noticing. It was as if a spell had been cast on Bort, putting him to sleep to dream a beautiful illusion of what should be important to him. Bort loved the people he'd met and devotedly made food for them. Bort enjoyed being a part of Lemnear. But as time passed, he felt lost, and his anxious heart bothered him. To compensate for these negative emotions, Bort distracted himself with video games, outings, festivals, and focused less on his quest to pursue his dreams, and piece back the shards of his memories.

One of the last things he had was his cooking. But tonight, that didn't do the trick. In fact, even in his love for making food, Bort found himself derailed from the original reason why he started cooking in the first place. Many townsfolk spoke highly of Bort's cooking abilities. Their acclaim swelled him with pride. Bort didn't realize he starved for more of that attention. He began to direct his craft by the praise of others as a substitute for true inner peace and not from within his heart. Bort's ego was dangerously inflated to the point that without the value given to him through flattery, he felt lesser, weak, and unimportant. He had become addicted to instant gratification.

Bort? You mean the master chef? He is a gem to Lemnear…

Bort's cooking is superb! There is nothing in Keevah like it!

I feel twenty years younger after eating Bort's delicious pancakes!

The praises of the townsfolk echoed in his mind. But this time, instead of feeling amped by their words, it made Bort recoil, and shake the memories from his head. For Bort, the comfort of being one of Lemnear's most celebrated chefs was an illusion, a mockery of why he made pancakes in the first place. They were his most cherished food in the whole wide world, and he loved being able to make the food that filled him with such happiness for friends and for others to share in the enjoyment. It was not because of what others thought of what he was, or how they saw him, or how they praised him; it was an expression for Bort: how he saw himself, the love and passion in his own heart, and the desire to share it without expectation with all who wanted.

Bort walked through the town with his eyes fixated on the cobblestone, deep in thought, followed by his squeaky wagon that kept rhythm with his steps. The sounds of Lemnear were distant to him, and the people that filled the plaza were like transparent phantoms, illusions that he had created. Everyone around him enjoyed themselves, contrasting his own emotions. Bort halted his pace and looked around. He felt so isolated and alone while everyone around him went on with their lives.

Bort looked back down at his feet; the serene nature of the town could no longer substitute for his discontent. He had to admit to himself then that it never had and had only ever served to preoccupy his emotions and distract from his purpose. It was much easier to do that than to put in the hard work needed to find the peace and understanding he sought from within his heart of hearts. The effort required to rediscover himself and realize his dreams was tremendously more than he was presently contributing. Distractions meant that he did not need to be outside of his comfort zone, he did not have to push past his own limits, and he did not have to truly experience the emotions that were uncomfortable but necessary to foster growth.

Bort tugged his wagon behind him and waddled onward. If this course of action continued, then his dreams would only ever remain just that: dreams. Nothing more than thoughts he had during sleep. The earlier morning lessons echoing over and over, teaching Bort how important it was to work to get where he wished to be — it was not enough to know it mentally, from his boat disaster; nor physically, as he'd struggled out from under Mr. Fluffy Feets; nor spiritually, from the advice given to him from his friends after admitting his failure; nor emotionally, as he processed it within himself. It could not be one or more of these revelations to spur the desire to transform and become more. It would take the unity of all four pillars of strength to understand and see through the clouded filter of his ego. That way, Bort could witness his intention with honest, crystalline clarity.

It was Bort's adventurer spirit that had been ringing through every fiber of his being. Not being listened to created the turmoil he felt. Bort raised his head up off the path beneath him and looked straight ahead, finding his resolve. Before long, Bort was at the town exit next to the Lemnear signpost for the Slug-Lug Express bus station. Not being the strongest reader, Bort examined the sign: "Welcome to Lemnear." Alongside it were signs displaying directions to the Fairy Ring Woods, Skello-Jack Forest, Lake Lemnear, and Stargazer Valley. The words were hard to sound out. Nevertheless, these had symbols that Bort was able to recognize the meanings of. There were so many different places just beyond the town he had never seen, and so many places he yearned to discover.

After a while looking at the signposts, Bort's gaze defaulted into peering up at the dream-filled night sky. The stars spilled through the heavens as the moons and far-off planets hung like colorful pancakes, faintly blurred by the mist in the atmosphere. It wasn't only the many places on this planet that he wanted to discover, but also entire worlds he wanted to see. Bort reached out towards the sky for what his entire being cried out for: becoming whole.

Bort cradled the heavens in his flipper, and his little walrus brain worked to find a solution for his new epiphany. He wanted so badly to return to what made him feel whole but was unsure how to achieve it. The familiar fire in his belly grew from the cinders of his troubled mind like a Phoenix rising from the ashes. Hot Dog came to mind, and at that moment, Bort decided to find a way, any way, to reach Lemnear's Glimmering Sparrow, to become the adventurer he, to a great extent, wanted to be. As that thought passed, one of the biggest and brightest shooting stars he'd ever seen flashed through the sky and fell into his open flipper, as if the stars above had acknowledged his decision and course of action.

Bort clenched his flipper, catching the shooting star, and smiled. He had made his decision, not wanting to put his dreams off any longer. Bort decided to begin asking for help or for ideas on how to get to the Spiral Cliffs. The snail-bus came to its scheduled pick up, waiting for Bort to board. Bort shook his head at the giant snail, waved, and headed back into town on foot. Bort figured, if he wanted to be an adventurer, then he would need all the training he could get.

CHAPTER XV

The Giant Horned Cow-Lady, Zankiras

The wind and watermills kept tempo with the chorus of crickets and frogs. Steam and smoke billowed up from street carts in the cool night air and filled the town with delectable aromas.

The lights and vivacious sounds of the marketplace were bustling. People gathered at shops and traded goods while street entertainers performed their shows and bards spun their melodic tales. The street carts were full of hungry patrons, while the center square played music with light and water displays. Though Lemnear's market was tiny compared to most those in other townships, and hard terrain made travel to the village difficult, its market was one of the best in the continent of Meliae.

The street carts, pubs, and taverns filled the night air with the aromas of delicious food. People crowded around the magiviewers and vidscreens that displayed news of other towns and advertisements for the local shops. Bort was amused by the marketplace at night and wanted to partake in all of it. However, he fought the urge to peruse the video-game, comic, food, and toy shops that littered the plaza. Bort had to focus! If anything were to help him build Hot Dog, he wouldn't find it there. He kept his attention on the woodworkers and metal shops, which had many unique and exciting items on display. But nothing seemed useful for rebuilding Hot Dog.

Bort nodded to himself and devised a plan. The local shops of Lemnear were full of master crafters. Although it is easy to find those with high skill, it was difficult to find a wide variety of shops. However, some of the traveling merchants and foreign shop keepers from different towns that had sprung up around the plaza could have just what he needed!

There was a well-known carpenter named Wyrran that made many of the marvelous homes, decorative bridges, and art pieces. But Bort had not seen him or his shop since he'd first arrived in Lemnear. Still, he decided to pay the shop a visit just in case before taking a stroll down Winder Realm Alley, where most of the foreign merchants had set up shop.

Bort was surprised to see the old carpenter lights on and hear the sounds of wood being worked in the far back of the shop. With a smile, Bort quickened his pace. He had so many questions for Wyrran, like which wood would be best used for a boat. How do you make a boat? Can a ship learn to do tricks? Do they like to eat slugs? So many more questions filled his mind, and Bort's excitement grew, knowing he was close to finding the answers.

Upon reaching the front counter of the shop, Bort peered up at it. As short as he was, seeing over the counter proved difficult, even standing atop his wagon. Bort reached up with his flippers and stood as tall as he could on his tippy toes. "Bo(E-excuse me.)rt," Bort said once he could press his head over the counter.

"Huh?" an annoyed voice bellowed from the bowels of the shop. A flowing torrent of long curly hair tossed about as the silhouetted carpenter turned in the direction of Bort's voice. A towering feminine figure stood upright, keeping her head bowed slightly forward so not to punch holes in the ceiling from the horns on her head.

She scanned the front booth, at first unable to see the little squashed brown walrus' face with two protruding flippers blending in with the dark wood counter-top. It was only when he blinked that she noticed his jeweled brown eyes peeking back at her. "Oh, a customer," she said, more soft-spoken. Her footfalls reverber-ated through the floor as she made her way towards Bort while removing her gloves. She ducked under the end of the ceiling and into the light, standing to her full height.

She was full-figured and massive, easily six times bigger than Bort. It was commonplace for the Minotaur kind to hold such a stature; however, even she was considered larger than average. Her horns projected from the sides of her head and formed the shape of a halberd, accentuated by long, curly honey-col-ored tresses that fell past her lower back. She sported blue denim overalls in front of a white long-sleeve shirt rolled up to her elbows. She placed her gloves in her tool belt and smiled. "How can I help ya, stranger?" she chirped. She leaned down and placed a forearm on the counter to meet Bort's gaze.

She sure wasn't Wyrran. She was unfamiliar to Bort and quite intimidating. Bort looked around the shop for the old carpenter. "Bo(I-is Wyrran still working here?)rt?" Bort said, confused.

"Wha—?" The carpenter said, ruffling her hair, unable to understand Bort.

Used to this, Bort became more animated, doing his best to interpret for the woman what he was asking for.

"Oh, Wyrran? After my apprenticeship with him, he moved his shop way out to the Shmakrees region with the rest of the gnomes. I am Zankiras, from the grasslands region of the Vylfera Kingdom," she said, pounding her chest, proud of her name and origin. Zankiras stood tall, hands on her hips, and looked around the marketplace. "You Lemnearians sure do business bizarrely. It's been difficult getting customers," she said in a terse tone.

Trading at the marketplace felt odd at first even for Bort, so he could relate. Although his past still eluded him, he knew some form of currency needed to be exchanged for goods and services. In Lemnear, however, this was not the case. The people of Lemnear used a trading system that heavily relied on honor and the desire to help one another. If one needed a house to be built, those who focused their craft on construction would erect the home, along with planners, engineers, and so on. In return, those builders would be able to prove the skill of their reputations and exercise their crafts and passions. The people of Lemnear saw the need for currency as a way to hinder people and have them do meaningless tasks that did nothing but aid in serving those richer and wasting the drive, dreams, and potential of those bound to labor. Lemnear was only one of a few places left in Keevah that did this. Most other regions and kingdoms worked off cash-based currency systems.

This made it challenging to arrange a trade with the other regions. However, because the people of these scarce towns grew in the careers they had chosen, the work, craftsmanship, services, and technology were almost always unparalleled. So, other nations and kingdoms struck commerce deals. Services or goods rendered could be paid with products or services of equal value, depending on the particular scales set by those governing territories. In turn, the merchants would send the commodities to their respective nations and would be paid in their currency.

Those from other kingdoms who were more passionate about their careers commonly adopted Lemnear's way of commerce, where they pursued their crafts, relentlessly. However, the governing nations from where they'd originated, quickly became aware of this trend. Not only would they lose skilled craftsmen or merchants, but they would lose the taxes they imposed on them as well. Thus today, many of the foreigners that did business in Lemnear were bounded by contracts, fees, and debt.

This was helpful for Lemnear as some of the goods from other towns had unique technologies Lemnear lacked, or synthetic materials unknown to Lemnear. But this did not come without its recourse. Repayment became difficult, as many of the goods called for substances that crossed different job classes or were hard to obtain. Oddly, numerous products the shops asked for were raw materials obtained from the forests and mountains. Although most people of Lemnear worked together to get the supplies, it began to foster thieves, con artists, crime, exploitation, and the illegal removal of precious resources of the forest.

Zankiras' face blushed red as she turned and ran her hand over a fresh-cut piece of wood. "But it is a small price to pay, if it means I get to work with the rare woods found here in Lemnear," she said with her passion for carving burning bright in her eyes. "With as much as I can learn here, no coin will ever pay back

the debt," she said.

Bort stared at her with a smile, able to understand that feeling. Zankiras felt Bort staring at her, and she cleared her throat, swallowing down her passionate tears. "So! What'll it be, big guy?" she said as she leaned on the counter down to Bort's level again.

Big guy? Bort thought as his face swelled with happiness. Bort still struggled to hold himself above the counter as he spoke with excitement. "Bo(It's nice to meet you, Zankiras. Yeah, I'm a really big guy. I'll grow to be big like you. I am Bort, and I wanna build Hot Dog!)rt!"

Zankiras raised an eyebrow at him and pointed down the street. "Nice to meet you, Bort, but yonder, that way, is the street cart—" she said in a dead tone.

"Bo(No! Hot Dog is the name of—)rt," Bort said as he slipped off the counter. For as big as she was, Zankiras' reflexes were fast; she snatched him by the scruff of his back and lifted him up to her face. "Bo(...My boat.)rt," he said. Bort put a flipper up, smiling big and bright. "Bo(Thanks for catching me, giant cow-horn lady, Zankiras. You saved my life.)rt."

"Hmm..." Zankiras grumbled. "A boat, you say?" she said, placing him on the counter.

Bort smushed a little as he was placed on the counter. "Bo(Yeah! Hot Dog! It's an adventurer's ship! Full of adventuring!)rt!" Bort said with as much grandeur as he could muster and waved his flippers in a big arch before dropping his flippers to his sides. "Bo(...and holes... lotsa lotsa holes... and it broke... and sunk... a barrel ran away too...)rt..." he said.

Zankiras folded her arms and brought her head down with a "Hmm...." Her mind filled with grandiose ideas and designs as she mumbled off what she needed. "Yes... Yes! I can make the bow of the ship like this... and the masts like so..." She trailed off and drew initial designs on a small notepad from her toolbelt.

Zankiras had worked through the ideas before thinking about what it would cost to build. "Hmm... This is gonna be expensive..." she said as she scratched her head with the back of her pencil.

Bort looked at her with a straight face. "Bo(I-I don't have any money... I can make you all the pancakes you want.)rt," he said wringing his flippers and noticed Zankiras stop her drawing. Bort looked at his flippers as he thought about it some more before meeting her gaze again. "Bo(I-I'll even give you my jar of extra-tasty shuggie slugs. I can even come and help somehow.)rt," he pleaded with every ounce of his candor.

Zankiras felt bad for Bort. She figured that he must be a chef in town that traded by making these meals called pancakes. Not only that: she was also passionate about being able to teach someone what she loved with all her heart, and here he wanted to learn. But how was she going to pay her contract from the Vylfera Kingdom without the goods required? She was torn between her obligation and the desire to build a boat. "Erm... well... I don't know if I can do that," she said in a meek voice.

Bort's little brain worked to find a solution. "Bo(I can bring you all the materials you need to build. I-I can be your sidekick. In fact, I would love to build the boat, too.)rt," Bort said with all his heart.

Zankiras' eyes dimmed as she thought about the debts she had and her obligation. With all the strength she could muster, she had to force out denying Bort. "I-I'm sorry..." is all she could say, staring into the big brown eyes of the little walrus.

Bort took in a deep breath. "Bo(No... It's okay.... I understand. Thanks anyway, Zankiras. It was nice to meet you.)rt," he said as he turned around and hopped off the counter onto his wagon then down to the ground. He turned back and smiled. "Bo(Come by and eat some pancakes sometime. And if you ever change your mind, please let me know, okay?)rt?"

Zankiras felt as if something inside her had died a little. "S-sure…" is all she was able to utter.

"Bo(See ya later!)rt," Bort said with a flipper in the air before he walked deeper into the market and disappeared into the crowd.

Zankiras stared at where Bort last was, all her passion drained from her face. "S-see ya," she said under her breath with her hand held in a frozen wave. With a deep sigh, she turned around and made her way back to the wood she'd been working with just minutes before. It felt as if it stared back at her with full disappointment. "But I had to," she said, knowing full well that she'd chosen business over her passion. She picked up the carving tool and was about to start work once again, but she could no longer feel the desire within her.

Zankiras' heart couldn't take it as it filled with anxiety. She'd changed her mind and ran to the counter. "H-hey! Bort!" she screamed out, but was only met with the crowd. With a heavy groan, she spun around, turned the shop lights off, and called it an early night.

CHAPTER XVI

The Mysterious Thoth and the Enchiridion

After talking to Zankiras, Bort left with a heavy heart. Yet, he was still filled with the determination to trudge forward and work for his dreams. For the moment, however, he decided to take a break. Bort visited a few food carts and eased his mind rambling through the maze-like plaza as he ate. Bort didn't have the best sense of direction, so he meandered down new paths and visited weird shops he'd never seen before. Bort's thoughts were not on being lost, but on the curious street vendors, street food, and the entertaining shows on the magiview screens.

After enjoying a puppet show, alongside the younger children, Bort got to his feet and decided it was time to go home for the night. But finding his way out of the marketplace was its own issue. Most of the shops were already closed, and only a few signs and pathway lights lit the area. Wandering down a quiet alley, the bustling sounds of the market faded, and soon the only sounds Bort heard were of his own footfalls and squeaky wagon.

The night air cooled as fog rolled in, signaling the late hours approaching. Bort had walked the market countless times but never this late. Being afraid of the dark, he hadn't realized how spooky even Lemnear could be. Worry began to etch itself on Bort's face, and he quickened his pace. He hoped to exit the market and be well on his way to his cozy bed. Just then, a giant gust of wind overtook the backstreet. Bracing himself against his wagon, Bort brought a flipper up to shield his eyes from flying debris. The gale was intense, causing him to turn away from the force of it, knocking him off balance. Bort hugged his wagon and held on with his eyes shut tightly, feeling his body lift off the ground.

As fast as it came, it settled. Once Bort felt safe enough, he opened his eyes and stood up. A few meters in front of him, a shop emerged from the misty night.

It was a dark blue tent that stood aloof. It was so inconspicuous that it was tough to distinguish between its wall and the darkness of midnight. Bort oh'ed and stared at the entrance of the tent, beguiled.

Curiosity got the best of him, and he pulled open the tent flap. The interior was deceptively bigger than it had looked from outside. Inside, many different-colored lights glistened, and sandalwood smoke hung thick in the air. Bort popped his head in with a short "Bort," making sure to keep most of his body outside so that if what he saw was scary, he could turn and flee.

There were bubbling potions, end to end walls of books, strange items, and magical weapons on display. It was pleasantly warm, and Bort found the smell of the incense relaxing.

"Bo(Hello?)rt?" Bort called out and waited for a response.

A long while passed without an answer. Bort's inquisitiveness bolstered his bravery, and he skittered the rest of his chubby body inside the tent along with his squeaky wagon. Fascinated by such a mysterious shop, Bort wandered deeper in, examining all around him with a flipper on his whiskered face.

Bort found all the bizarre items in this store incredible. He had never seen so many funny-looking things, and they had so many different odors! As Bort smelled a clunky shoe, a glint of something powerful caught his attention. Behind a counter in the middle wall was displayed a spectacular glistening round shield on a pedestal. Bort's eyes widened, and before he knew it, his legs had brought him right next to it. As he focused on the shield, a deep, booming voice echoed throughout the tent, shattering Bort's stupor.

"Welcome, wandering soul! Welcome to the Theurgic Emporium of Wondrous Phenomena. I am Thoth, the shopkeeper and steward of this place, and it is my highest pleasure to provide for you in seeking out the hunger of your core."

Bort screamed, surprised. Panic rushed through his nervous system, and with flippers high in the air, he darted off behind a tall column of mage hats. Noticing he abandoned his wagon companion; an icy finger of fear ran down Bort's back. He shot out like a beam of brown lightning, retrieved his wagon, and zipped back behind the headwear.

"No need to fear. I mean you no harm," the disembodied voice who called itself Thoth chuckled.

After a long and silent pause, Bort's head emerged from behind the pillar. Having knocked off a dark-blue wizard's hat from the rack in his haste, it now rested cockeyed on Bort's head, covering one of his eyes.

What Bort thought was a silhouette of a statue began to move, while two piercing pale-blue eyes shone from it. The sound of a book shutting boomed from its direction, and the silhouette rose from a squat.

"Forgive my late introduction. I did not notice you enter my shop," Thoth said.

The shadow moved at a glacial pace towards Bort as it stepped into the light. A regal-looking, well-groomed baboon clad in pristine white fur stood ahead of Bort. His dark-colored hairless face accented his azure pupil-less eyes. His long tail swayed behind him at a languid rhythm. The bells and pendants that hung off his garb and staff he held tolled in tempo to his steps. Thoth had a calmness in his manner. He carried with him a noble, powerful, and enigmatic aura that compelled Bort's nerves to settle. Bort ducked back behind the hat rack to grab his wagon and walked into sight.

"Bo(I said hello.)rt," Bort said.

Thoth reeled back with a hint of embarrassment and looked away. "Did you, now? Perhaps I have grown more complacent in the many years I have been here," he said more to himself than to Bort. Thoth faced Bort once more, and with a slight bow of his head, said, "Forgive my rudeness. It is very uncommon to have visitors here nowadays."

Thoth stepped closer to Bort, intrigued with the diminutive walrus. "Hm…" Thoth muttered pensively, charmed by Bort's aura. "Why, aren't you a curious fellow. You are very unlike the rest of the beings of Lemnear. What is your name?"

"Bort," Bort said with a flipper in the air and a smile on his face. His entire demeanor had changed, excited to meet someone new.

"I see," Thoth said, circling Bort and assessing him. "Pleasure to meet you… Bort," he said with a deliberate pause before speaking his name. "Very curious, indeed," Thoth said, studying Bort. after an awkward silence, Thoth turned and made his way back into the shadows of the shop. Bort watched him disappear into the darkness before Thoth's voice bellowed, "You are unlike those in this realm. Where is it you are from, Master Bort?"

Bort put his flipper down and stared in Thoth's direction "Bo(I don't remember. I hit my head real good before I got here a whole year ago. All I can remember is playing around Lemnear when Garlic found me.)rt," he said. Bort's gaze wandered around the shop before he clasped his flippers in front of him. "Bo(Sometimes… I remember stuff. Like people, feelings, places, and I know how to do certain things. When I think about them for a long time or try super hard to remember, it hurts my head. Like when I trip and fall down the stairs kinda hurt. But mostly, the remembories come when I taste or smell something familiar, or something happens that reminds me of a feeling. Other times, I'll boop my head, and I see a piece of my memory. And then I feel sad, like I'm missing someone, or that I need to be looking for something very important to me.)rt," he said in a brittle voice.

As Bort wove the tale of his amnesia, Thoth reemerged from the depths of the shop with a grave expression. "And so, your origins remain a puzzle to you."

Bort nodded. "Bo(Yes... I still look for traces of them. Sometimes in my dreams, I think they are my rememborles, remembering. So when I wake up in the morning...)rt..." Bort said and held a deep breath. He then covered his ears with his flippers, squeezing his head, and shut his eyes tightly. "Bo(I go like this, so they don't escape through my head or face, and I try to remember and remember.)rt," Bort said before trembling then turning blue, and he exhaled with a great puff of air.

Bort let his flippers fall limp to his sides and gazed at the floor. "Bo(I wanna write them down, but I'm still learning how.)rt," Bort said, looking up at Thoth. "Bo(So, I usually make lots of drawings of 'em with my crayons!)rt!" Bort said with excitement, throwing his flippers in the air.

Thoth chuckled at the animated walrus. "I see," he said, giving Bort his full attention. "Even over-encumbered with so much strife, you manage to remain in good spirits." Thoth signaled Bort to follow him. "You see, Master Bort, it is not very often I get visitors these days. It takes a certain... element that lays within a person's spirit for the Theurgic Emporium of Wondrous Phenomena to reveal itself, much less allow someone to enter it. Beyond the enigma within you, the might and drive of your heart explains why you were able to discover it so easily."

Bort gasped and ran up to Thoth. "Bo(Oh! Like the chocolate custard frog-horn buns?")rt? Bort said. Before allowing Thoth a chance to respond, Bort's face grew passionate and he continued, "Bo(Some say the froghorn bun maker never comes out on cloudy days. The street cart only appears in the misty evenings, and it's never in the same place twice! It is said that one om-nom of it is so good you can see the flavors!)rt!" Bort said and raised his free flipper, clenching it into a fist. "Bo(One day, I will find the Froghorn bun maker, and I will eat the delicious pastry and become super-Bort!)rt!" Bort vowed.

Thoth was shocked. Did his shop just get compared to the legendary Frog-horn bun maker? Worst of all, Thoth could not help but feel a hint of jealousy and pride at the way Bort made it sound; yet, it also made him salivate! Thoth cleared his throat. "Ahem! Erm, yes... Something like that," he said flustered.

Bort's eyes grew wide. "Bo(Amazing! I made it to a secret place! I unlocked a Bort trophy!)rt!" he shouted, raising his flippers and dancing. "Bo(Save game! Save game!)rt!" Bort added, playing the video game in his head.

Thoth stopped in his path and grinned. Noticing how excited Bort was to find the shop strengthened his spirit, and it felt like eons since he had sensed such a force. "Ahem. Shall we?" Thoth said, watching Bort celebrate. Bort waved, grabbed his wagon, and followed once more.

"There was once a time where auras like yours were commonplace. So much so that my shop was perused by countless beings from across the realms. Alas, that light has dimmed and seems to be coming to pass. Now, my shop is but a relic of what it once was, a fable only known by mages, wizards, alchemists, and sorcerers," Thoth said with a hint of sorrow as he grazed his hand over the wall of books they passed by.

"This place holds many curious things. Everything you see around you has spirits all their own," Thoth said and looked around his shop. "I can hear their whispers and whose hearts they call out for that intrigue them," Thoth said.

Thoth led the way further and further into the emporium. They walked by many unusual items, such as glowing bottles, sparkling bags of powders, power-charged stones infused with elements like water, fire, storm, earth, gale, and the like, along with armaments that resonated as Bort walked by them.

Bort did his best to be respectful and listen with his full attention. However, everything inside the shop distracted him, especially walking by the various colored potion bottles that distorted their reflections. While Bort followed Thoth, their mirror images in each vial, changed their shapes. In some, they appeared skinny, others tall, and some of them mixed them up like a whirlpool. Thoth continued speaking while Bort stifled his laughter. "Hmm," Thoth muttered and smirked, "there are many relics here that call out to you, Bort, but there is one spirit I hear the loudest."

They made their way through a corridor with an ornate wooden door at its end.

"Ahh, yes. In here," Thoth said and grabbed the door handle. "Very interesting, indeed," he said and looked behind him with an incredulous glare at Bort.

Thoth pulled the door open, whereupon a rush of fresh air and multicolored lights enveloped Bort. Bort looked up at Thoth, who held the door and nodded at him to continue forward. Bort looked back into the passageway and gulped before stepping past the threshold of the mysterious room. The ground was black as night. Thinking he would fall through the floor, Bort held onto the edges of the doorframe, gingerly testing the ground with his foot.

"There is nothing to fear," Thoth said with laughter.

Bort turned and looked at Thoth, who gestured Bort into the room. Bort looked back at the ground and exhaled. His flipper hit the floor with commitment, which caused a ripple throughout the room, and glowing webbing sank into the pitch-black deck. Enchanted, Bort kept his eyes on his feet, watching the ripples coming from his steps. In the infinite space below Bort, he could see a litany of stars, nebulas, and distant galaxies. The same was all around him, save for mountains and forests that seemed to be far off in the distance floating in the eternal nothing. Placed all around him were objects Bort had never seen, and they looked unbelievably old. Some were recognizable, such as mirrors, obelisks, statues, and weapons, but others were extraordinarily alien.

Thoth turned and looked to Bort. "Here is where enigmas from the far-off corners of the world and from distant realms well outside our comprehension have been kept for ages," he said. "You are the one who makes the town smell of berries and sweetness, are you not?" He then placed his hand over an ancient tome on a pedestal made of glowing granite that harbored different plant life, tiny creatures, and was surrounded by trees.

"Bo(Hmm? Y-you mean my pancakes? Yeah, That's me. You should come and have one sometime)rt," Bort managed to say, still mesmerized by the enigmatic room.

Thoth gently brushed aside the growth and ushered off the little beings that rested atop the book before removing it from its pedestal. Thoth brought the manuscript near his face and blew at the cover, dusting off eons of slumber from the tome and awakening it. Thoth smiled at the book, the look on his face was genuine, as if he saw a friend he hadn't seen in years. He turned to Bort, who looked back at him, eyes full of bright dreams and endless wonder.

"I believe this spirit is eager to meet yours," Thoth said and handed Bort the old book. Bort held the volume, feeling the weight of what was bestowed upon him and the unrelenting curiosity to see what the pages contained.

"This book has gone by many names. But I have only ever known it by one. The Enchiridion," Thoth said. "The Enchiridion is eager to meet you, young master, Bort."

Bort examined the cover. Its design was simple; leather and metal with a lapis lazuli in the center. A serpent-like creature wove itself into a knot just underneath the stone, and a button-lock held the tome closed. The book was enormous, almost the same height as Bort and half as thick!

"Bo(Whoa...)rt..." Bort said in awe and admired the tome. Bort pressed the lock, and the mechanism engaged, popping out the strap. The book began to glow with a hum. He pulled the cover open, and light erupted into the room along with orbs of magic and swirling gales of energy. Bort did his best to hold onto the manuscript and shield his eyes from the intense brilliance. But the Enchiridion soon broke free from his flippers, encasing itself in a pillar of light. The Enchiridion's cover began to animate. The serpent began to crawl through the cover of the tome, unlocking the metal bits, causing them to shift. The book was as much mechanical as it was magical, by the sounds of cogs turning and whirring while the tome glimmered with spiritual script etching onto it.

Emblems and pictographs of Bort appeared around the corners of the Enchiridion. The Serpent wove around the center of the book, which resembled a solitary trunk with two sets of branches above and below. One set of branches was full of leaves, and the other was empty of them, resembling roots. The lapis lazuli shattered into twelve different-colored stones that found their places encircling the great tree, and behind the tree and gems were three different-colored circles

that meshed in the middle where the trunk was.

Watching from the side, a smile had grown over Thoth's face. "It really has been too long," he said to himself.

Once the Enchiridion imprinted on its chosen master, it drifted down in front of Bort, who plucked it from the air with great care, and the pillar of light faded into darkness. Awestruck, Bort opened the book and browsed through the pages, careful not to damage them. Many of them were smudged and scarcely legible, and some pages were torn from their binding. It was an old book, after all. Aside from that, the tome was full of writing with depictions of different kinds of flora, fauna, locations, and many other fascinating things. There was a chapter of ingredients, and raw materials took up about a third of the book. Where these items could be found were indicated on a map that dotted across the regions of Keevah, along with the time to pick them and rankings of their rarity.

"It seems that the Enchiridion likes you already," Thoth said. "As you can see, it has seen better days. I hope you can help it restore itself to its former glory as it assists you with yours. All the while developing an unbreakable bond," he said.

Bort turned to Thoth, unsure as to how to interpret his cryptic words, but he understood the weight they carried. With that, Bort closed his eyes, committing himself to his newfound responsibility, and nodded before returning to the book. "Bo(Ooh)rt…" he said, amazed. His pupils dilated as he took in every detail of the map and studied it. He recognized the region of Lemnear and slapped his flipper onto the book, pointing it out. "Bo(Look, look, look! It's Lemnear!)rt!" he shouted in excitement and showed Thoth the map. Bort held it out for a moment before bringing it back and sticking his nose in it to get a better look.

Thoth chuckled under his breath and positioned himself at Bort's shoulder. "And you are in luck, Master Bort! The Lemnear region is rampant with resources, and its mountain ranges bountiful with many mysteries to discover. The same goes for the whole of Meliae," Thoth said and laid a hand on Bort's shoulder.

Bort brought his face out from the book and looked at Thoth starry-eyed. "Yes, like this specific ingredient," Thoth said, removing his hand from Bort's shoulder. He turned the pages to the comprehensive list of ingredients and tapped on an odd-looking depiction of a mushroom. Bort stuffed his face back into the book, while Thoth walked around the room and spoke. "It's said to grow just beyond the Skello-Jack forest. However, it is a rare one, undeniably. Even master mushroom hunters have difficulty acquiring it. This peculiar ingredient is succulent and sweet. It tastes like a berry in nature, but no blueberry or strawberry can contend with it. I cannot even fathom what wondrous dishes you can create with this," Thoth said, sparking the dormant energy welling inside the fluffy walrus.

Thoth, so compelled by his own speech, failed to hear Bort's frantic thanks and fair-winds as he made a hasty exit. As Thoth turned to face Bort, he was met only with the afterimage of the walrus, the dark blue mage's hat sailing to the floor, and trailing dust was all that remained as evidence of his departure.

"Ahem! Erm, Master Bort?" Thoth said and followed Bort's path. Thoth made it to the front of his shop just in time to see the tent flapping, accompanied by sounds of flippers against the road and wagon squeaks trailing off into the distance. Thoth let out a chuckle, closed his eyes, and returned to his shop. "I enjoyed our first encounter. May it be the beginning of many. See you again very soon, young master, Bort."

CHAPTER XVII

I'll Rise from the Ashes Like the Phoenix! If Only I Could Read!

Bort raced back home through the market. Thoth had reawakened his passion to be the best chef he could be. The Enchiridion grew an appetite to uncover never-before-seen ingredients. He was so excited to have been given the tome filled with pages upon pages of rare and legendary ingredients, all at his fingertips! That chapter alone was about as thick as his tusk! Bort looked back into his wagon. Was it all just some dream that he'd happened across Thoth and the Enchiridion? He needed to make sure he'd hadn't been trying some new disgusting wonder back home and had passed out in some fever dream. Yet, there it was, the Enchiridion bouncing in his cart.

Bort shook with excitement as his mind raced. How many ingredients were out there? What did they taste like? How many were around Lemnear alone? What did they look like? Bort barreled home so that he could study the book at length. His desire to cook wasn't the only thing to be resurrected, but he could perhaps enhance his super-not-so-secret secret adventure-hero training program by seeking out rare ingredients!

However...

Bort dug his heels into the path, and glowered off into nothing.

"Bo(Stupid reading.)rt," Bort grumbled to himself and blew a raspberry.

Bort knew how to read. Well, maybe not all the words, nor quite well, and had to sound it out most of the time. It was something Bort felt he'd been just learning even before his amnesia. When he lived with Garlic, he always rummaged through her library of books when Garlic sat down to study her magic or concoct new recipes for her apothecary. Bort would grow so bored that even drawing and coloring would feel dull. Before he was able to get his flippers on toys and video games, he would scour her books, which proved to be the best thing he had ever done.

Bort pulled out a book and opened it. The words looked like scribbles to him and were confusing. His face contorted into anguish, trying to make sense of what he was looking at. He tilted the book back and forth and craned his neck trying to decipher the squiggles. He rotated the book until it was upside down; it still did not make sense but looked more legible at this angle.

Bort heard a chuckle come from Garlic's desk. He looked up and saw her staring at him. Embarrassed, Bort hmphed and turned his back to her, making an "ah-hah" sound as if he'd figured out the book. It was all show, of course, and Garlic knew it. She shook her head, smiling, and walked up to Bort.

Garlic flipped the book right-side up. "There you go, Bort. See? Like this. Now, watch carefully, it reads, like this..." she said and traced her index finger from left to right and down the page where Bort followed with his eyes, attentive to her tutorial on the sly. Garlic stood upright, her hands on her hips. "Raehern Erohan Vesstan's Wonderous Collections of Myths, Might, and Magic, Volume One, huh? Not a bad choice at all!" She pet his head and watched him attempt to read the book.

Bort looked the book up and down for a moment before side-glancing Garlic and huddling over the volume. Garlic raised her hands and smirked, walking back to her desk, letting Bort discover the book on his own. Moments passed in silence; all the while Garlic wrote out measured equations while Bort flipped through the pages of the manuscript.

Bort found the illustrations of the book amazing. Each of them contained heroes, swords, magic, and monsters, all of which excited him. He wanted so badly to know what the pictures meant and did his best to decipher the words. But after his show of arrogance, he didn't know the best way to ask for Garlic's help, which he now regretted. He scanned through the pages until he found something familiar! At last! Now was his big chance!

"Bo(G...)rt," he said, getting Garlic's attention.

She paused for a moment to stare up at him, and he returned her gaze with a smile. He turned the next page and traced his flipper over the page like Garlic had moments earlier. "Bo(...G!)rt," he said again, immensely proud of himself.

Garlic set her pen down, smiled, placing her chin on her hands, and watched Bort scroll through the sentences calling out every letter g he could find. She giggled and walked over to Bort, who had his face plastered in the book, setting up the recliner next to him.

She snatched the volume from his flippers and plopped down into the seat. "Okay, mister, there is no way you will go another day not knowing how to fully read. Come'ere," she said and raised the book so he could sneak underneath it to sit between the book and Garlic. "Now pay close attention. I'll read you the tale first, and then we will go over it, okay, Bort?" Garlic said as Bort nodded, settling between the book and his dear friend.

Garlic recited the tale, captivating Bort's imagination right away. "During the dark days of the Ainalie and before the spark of the Fallen War was a young maiden named Lemnear Risai T'Leia…"

PRESENT DAY

Bort's mind returned to the present moment where the lightbulb in his head flickered and turned on.

Garlic!

Garlic could help him read the Enchiridion! Bort was lucky enough to find himself back at the market square and veered for Garlic's apothecary.

CHAPTER XVIII

What's a Rekka Mushroom?

Bort creaked the door open to Garlic's house and popped his head in. As per usual in the late evenings at the apothecary, Garlic's potion making was in full swing. The sounds of cauldrons bubbled and boiled, and mana infused crystals hummed while resonating eerie light. Foggy mystic spell circles were scribed in the air as well as on the ground. Pots boiled under fires, and books laid strewn about, while the rhythmic sound of ticking clocks kept tempo with the hum of oscillating magical energy. The scent of medicinal herbs and cooking was pleasing, albeit pungent.

The unique sights, sounds, and smells imprinted on Bort the first time he'd set foot in Garlic's house. Now every time he did, it brought back the fond and comforting memory of first meeting her. He felt that if he were to forget everything all over again, these things alone would help him remember his dear friend.

Bort smiled and waddled in towards the front desk with the giant book in hand. He slid the Enchiridion on top of the counter before commencing his ritual of summoning Garlic from her work. The desk was too high for Bort to look over, and calling out to Garlic never got her attention. There was a bell on the table that Bort reached a grubby flipper out to, groping around for it, as usual, to no avail. Grasping at the front of the counter, Bort began jumping up and down, catching glimpses of the bell. Bort struck it as many times as he could before gravity reclaimed him, all the while calling out to get Garlic's attention.

"Huh? Bort?" Garlic's voice came from the back room. Garlic leaned backward, looking past the wall towards her shop where she saw Bort's head bobbing up and down behind the counter. Garlic wiped her hands and bolted over towards Bort and dove over the desk. She reached out for Bort intending to give the soft walrus a big hug. Bort stepped back and extended his flippers, bracing himself. Garlic scooped him up and twirled around with him, pressing her cheek into his, and hugged his soft, warm body snugly against hers. It would've looked aggressive to anyone on the outside, but Bort loved the affection she showed him and nuzzled her back, squeezing his cheek back into hers.

"I didn't expect you to come over today, especially so late! What a pleasant surprise! You here to practice some magic?" she said as she put him down, holding his shoulders.

"Bo(Oh! That sounds fun! But I really came here to show you this.)rt," he said as he turned around, picking up the Enchiridion, and showed it to Garlic.

"Ha-ha! Oh? You want me to read you a story?" she assumed before examining the book.

"Bo(I mean, yes! Always! We still haven't gone through Raehern Erohan Vesstan's Wonderous Collections of Myths, Might, and Magic, Volume Four! But right now, you gotta take a look at this!)rt!" he said with excitement and bounced in place.

"Hmm." Garlic examined the Enchiridion. "A spell book? No..." she said to herself and touched the tome. Its cover was old, made with materials she was unfamiliar with. Not to mention, she saw little depictions of Bort on it. "Definitely magical... but what is it?" she asked herself.

Bort explained to Garlic what had happened to him earlier: his encounter with the weird store, and the mysterious stranger who called himself Thoth. Garlic had never heard of the Theurgic Emporium of Wondrous Phenomena being in Lemnear before, but the name of the shop and the stranger named Thoth was annoyingly familiar.

"I swear I have read about that somewhere before," Garlic said. She placed a hand on her hip and held her chin as she looked up, searching for the answer.

Garlic shrugged and decided to research it some other time. "Anyway, what is in the book?" she said after a short moment, turning her attention back to Bort.

"Bo(The Enchiridion will show me all the things! See?)rt?" Bort said. He opened the book and flipped through the pages to the ingredients chapter. Garlic caught glimpses of rare and legendary ingredients she had only read about in her medicinal-herb books. Many that she was able to recognize were said to have gone extinct long ago. "What? How can this be?" Garlic said in a hushed voice.

Bort looked down at the book for a long while before turning to Garlic with a vulnerable expression. "Bo(I'm still stinky at reading. I need help. Can you read it to me? Then help me to read it for myself? Please.)rt," he borted out with conviction.

It was a big step for him. Bort remembered his lesson about doing whatever it took to lead his dreams. Putting aside his pride, he needed help. Now was not the time to let ego prevail over his higher purpose; he had to ask for help with something that challenged him to a great extent.

But Garlic, unaware of his deeper plight, tested his conviction. "By the Golwen Gods! You are actually asking for me to help you read?" Garlic teased and dramatically put the back of her hand to her forehead and fanned herself. "I must be dreaming! Hm, I'm feeling faint!" she said with a smirk.

Bort's face drooped with annoyance, and he grimaced with a thousand-yard gaze as Garlic continued with her theatrics. Nevertheless, Bort knew he'd had it coming, and this was perhaps the first payment of many installments to come. Alas, he swallowed his pride. "Bo (Oh, ha-ha. Very funny, but will you, please?) rt?" he said in earnest.

Garlic looked over at Bort, noticed the sincerity in his demeanor, and dropped the act. Without another question, she gave Bort a loving smile. "Of course, I'll help you," she said.

Bort's face lit up with excitement and relief.

They moved to the recliner and took their seats, this time with Bort holding the book open. Garlic looked over his shoulder and placed a finger on the text, waiting for him to begin. "Bor... Bort-Bor, Bort. Bort... Boooor..." Bort began, focused on sounding out the words just right, following Garlic's finger with his face just inches from the book.

Seeing his struggle, Garlic chimed in. "Shroom."

"Bort."

"Good Job! Now, all together."

Garlic repeated the word slowly with Bort. "Bort-Bort."

"Mushroom," they said in sync.

Garlic's expression grew serious as she read ahead of her slower friend. Her eyes darted over the words, and the look on her face grew thrilled.

"By the Golweness!" she exclaimed and nudged her face next to Bort's. Pressed cheek to cheek with Bort, Garlic started reading ahead of Bort, who was still reading at his own pace, doing his best to ignore Garlic. He shot nervous glances to Garlic as he worked on his reading skills. "Found deep past the living towers of emerald hue, they only grow on pale twin sisters rising under the watch of Cormacolindo, in the House of Afarienrya..."

Bort was reading past "emerald hue" while Garlic read on. Bort began to sweat, trying to catch up to Garlic as she continued, "...beyond the ancient forest, upon the edge zone of the wandering thunderlands, sprouts neither berry nor bush, but a toadstool sweet as honey." Garlic paused for a long moment as sparks flared in her eyes. The pause was much needed for Bort to catch up, and they were both able to say it, almost in sync, with Bort lagging a few syllables behind.

"The rekka mushroom!" they said aloud. Garlic looked up with an expression of disbelief. Bort stretched his head up high, proud that he read the words thoroughly and properly all by himself.

"Bo(What's a rekka?)rt?" Bort said, turning to Garlic.

Garlic pet his head as she explained, scarcely containing herself. "I know only of it through arcane medicinal potions and spell books. The rekka mushroom has many healing properties and uses for spell making. It was highly sought after by shamans and healers to cure many ailments of the digestive system and apparently did wonders to regenerate cells in the body. It was said to taste so sweet that it was a delicacy for medicinal cooking. But because of that, it is widely believed to have been eaten into extinction. It hasn't been seen for a long time now. But everything I have read says it doesn't even grow in this region. I cannot believe it! If what this book contains is true, then—" she cut herself off, and her eyes darted back and forth as a torrent of thoughts flooded her mind.

She grabbed Bort by his shoulders and looked deeply into his eyes. "Bort! The Enchiridion is describing the Skello-Jack Forest and the Huntress constellation during the Dual Plenus Moons phase! The Huntress constellation is during this season, and the Dual Plenus Moons are in five days! We have to go find it!" she said with a squeal, hugging Bort tightly.

"Bo(Yay!)rt!" he exclaimed, throwing his flippers in the air in agreement, also unable to contain his excitement.

"There is so much I need to do to prepare! Ah!" Garlic said as she ran off to prepare the processes to compound the fabled ingredient.

"Bo(Yeah! Me, too! Me, too!)rt!" Bort exclaimed as he danced in place.

"Then it's settled. We will begin searching for the rekka mushroom," Garlic said, "and don't you worry. Believe it or not, I've done this kind of work before, ya know," she added, nudging Bort with a wink. "We will find it in no time!"

Garlic's words brought Bort's confidence up. Knowing that his friend would head out to help him find the mushroom made him feel secure. He was so excited that he closed the Enchiridion and prepared to head back to his house. "Bo(Okay, I better get some rest. It'll be a big day tomorrow.)rt," he said.

Garlic smiled. "That's right. I have so much to prepare. But I think I can get it all done," she said, working it out in her head. She turned to Bort and waived fairwinds as he returned the gesture.

He raced back home to try and get some rest. He would need all his strength if he were to go foraging for mushrooms and experiment with new dishes.

CHAPTER XIX

The Jerboa, the Monster, and the Mushroom

Once Bort made it home, he began formulating ingredients and soup stocks to experiment with the flavor of the rekka mushroom right away. He looked for any empty jars he could find to house the mushroom and made space for it on his shelves. Even though the rekka mushroom might not have even existed anymore, Bort believed with all his heart that it did, and he was going to find it. Bort started looking through some of the mysterious cabinets he hadn't gone through yet. Bort's mind was so preoccupied thinking about the rekka mushroom that he was searching on autopilot. Bort pulled out a stool and climbed up to where he then rifled through the forgotten shelves above his stove. Lost in his thoughts, Bort pulled open the cabinet doors covered in spiderwebs. Triggering a slumbering colony of cryptkeep bats to fly out from it, dislodging a horned skull that shifted down, its jaw agape, revealing numerous rows of teeth.

"Bort!" Bort screamed, his heart just about jumped out of his mouth as he shut the cabinet and braced his back against it. Bort watched the cryptkeep bats circle and click around in his restaurant. Just as Bort was about to raise his flippers to his head and panic, the front door chimed and opened. An older Nyarro entered and ducked in time to watch the colony of cryptkeeps flutter into the night.

"Oi! Fair suck of the sav! Cryptkeep bats! Heaps of'em! What are they doin' round here?" The Nyarro said, dusting himself off and watching the bats fly off into the night.

Relieved, Bort exhaled. "Bo(Phew! Thanks for saving my life, Myco!)rt," he said.

Myco's big, long ears twitched, picking up Bort's words. Myco turned to face him with a big smile. "G'day, Bort. Were those yer pets? I haven't seen cryptkeeps, not within cooee," he said, taking off his shoes, preparing to enter the restaurant.

Nyarros were a race of rodentlike beings that populated the southern hemisphere of Keevah. Myco looked like a jerboa with long ears and a long tail. His fur was black with blue patterns and stripes. He was usually dressed in cargo pants, a multi-pocketed button-up shirt, and his trademark slouch hat with one side pinned up, revealing his rank in the mushroom-hunters' guild. Myco has been Lemnear's lead mushroom expert for decades, and because Lemnear allowed him to further his craft, Myco was one of the best in the land when it came to mushrooms. He was a tender yet boisterous and ornery old jerboa; stubborn and quick to turn ill-tempered.

"Bo(I haven't explored every inch of this place yet, so there are still many mysteries. Like cryptkeep bats.)rt," Bort said and climbed down the stool.

"Ah," Myco acknowledged, brushing off the incident. "It's been a Buckley's chance for me to grab a bite. I know it's late, but I was hopin' to get a fair dinkum meal if you are still servin'?" Myco said, taking a seat by the counter.

Bort didn't plan on serving tonight. In fact, the next thing on his list was to make a 'Sorry, we are closed' sign. However, of all people to show up for a late-night meal, it happened to be Myco, the mushroom master!

Myco was usually too entrenched with his research to come out to eat. Yet whenever he did find the time, it was commonplace to spot him at Bort's Pancake Shop.

Who better to ask than a great mushroom hunter about the rekka mushroom and its possible existence just beyond the Skello-Jack Forest?

"Bo(Wow! Perfect timing! What'll it be?)rt?" Bort asked, and Myco placed an order for a full stack of berrydew pancakes in a sweet honey-crisp applejack glaze. Bort began to prepare the ingredients. "Bo(Hey Myco? What do you know about the rekka mushroom?)rt?" Bort asked as he cracked an egg into his batter.

"The rekka mushroom? Oi, mate, I know of it. I have only seen that beaut once in me youth," Myco said. "Ha-ha! I'm surprised you know about it, lad."

"Bo(Yeah, I just learned about it today.)rt," Bort replied and poured his mixture into a hot pan. The sound of sizzling batter accompanied the delicious aroma.

"Ah! Well, good on ya, lad! I first had a taste of one when I was an ankle-bit-er. I wasn't much older than you," Myco said. "When I was first studyin' about mushrooms, we were told that the rekka mushroom was found far, far away from Meliae. Even in those times, the arguments were whether it was already extinct or just extremely endangered," Myco reminisced while Bort flipped the pancakes.

"Me granddad lived in Lemnear and fell ill shortly after my graduation. So, I decided to come here and take care of him. One day, I shared what I had learned about the rekka mushroom with me granddad, and he perked up. 'That's the ticket!' he said, and in his weakened state, he ventured into the woop-woop," Myco explained.

Bort gave Myco his undivided attention as he finished making the pancakes, drizzling the glaze over them, and served them to Myco.

"Oi! Ta lad! They look sweet as," he said and took a few heaping mouthfuls before he continued his story. "Me granddad returned later that night, and in his hands were small rekka mushrooms." He paused to take another bite of his pancakes.

Bort was engrossed with the story. "Bo(Whoa! What did they taste like?)rt?" Bort asked, standing on his tippy toes with his eyes locked on Myco.

Myco smirked and swallowed. "Oi. Now, Bort, it was unlike anything I have ever eaten in me life! And me granddad woke the next morning feeling strong and fit. It's all thanks to him that I know so much about the rekka mushroom. However, even though he had told me where to find them, I haven't seen another ever since. We walked the woop-woop many times after that but never found another rekka mushroom." Myco's voice grew somber toward the end of his tale. "If we had found some, I am sure I would have been able to be with me granddad a few more years... It was after that when I decided to hunt for the rekka mushroom and research each of the conditions from where they were found."

In between his bites, Myco continued his story while Bort kept his tea filled and cleaned his kitchen.

"I scoured over many places around here and read every piece of literature that even mentioned the rekka mushroom in the mushroom-hunter guilds. It was strange to read that it was once so common a mushroom found everywhere. But

everything I read kept leading me back to this continent, Meliae. It was a long while, but I believe it to be somewhere close to Lemnear," Myco concluded.

Bort became excited from Myco's verification on the whereabouts of the rekka mushroom. "Bo(Yeah! Yeah! Yeah! The Enchiridion said that the rekka mushroom is in the Skello-Jack Forest!)rt!" he said.

Cough! Cough! Cough! Myco struggled to wash down his premature swallow with a glass of water. "Oi... The Skello-Jack forest?" he exclaimed, pushing up from his seat and leaning closely into Bort, interrupting his cleaning. "Oi! That's bloody interestin'! It seems I was on the right track, after all! Ace!" Myco said to himself, dispelling any doubt he'd had. "But it's all bulldust now. There's a bonzer of a monster in those woods!" Myco leaned in even closer to Bort with a look on his face of pure terror.

"I've been out in the thick of it, I have, about the time you showed up here, hot on the trail of the rekka mushroom you're talkin' about. When I took a tumble 'n landed on me arse. As I got back to me feet, I saw a silhouette of shadows rise from the forest floor, and two large glowing eyes as big as these pancakes here shone right through me soul!" Myco said as animated as ever. "If I hadn't been a dunny-rat, I would've been its dinner," he said. "When I came back, no one believed me. Pig's arse! But I tell you, mate, those woods are cursed, and a terrible monster roams those parts."

Bort was huddled and shaking as Myco was now leaning deep into Bort's face. Bort squeezed inside himself as much as he could, like a tortoise trying to hide in its shell, while grasping a ladle and bottle of honey, hugging them closely for protection. "Bo(Yuh... You mean... like a demogorgon?)rt?" Bort said, recalling the terrible monster he'd faced in Super Adventure Jump Hero RPG I: A Heroes Tale.

"Aye, lad! Just like a demogorgon," Myco said, wide-eyed and nodding his head ominously.

Bort gulped hard with shaky legs, tucked his head as far down into his shoulders as he could get it, and slowly returned to his tasks. After Myco finished his meal, he thanked Bort and apologized for the late intrusion as he made his exit. Bort was a little disheartened, but what if the old jerboa had mistaken seeing the two moons through the forest for eyes? Or for the silhouette of a scurrying animal? But what if he was telling the truth? Bort became full of questions as he finished up and prepared for bed.

No matter how much he thought about it, the desire to find this rare mushroom overtook any doubt or fear Bort may have now had. Bort walked up the stairs and into his room, where models hung from the roof, posters were plastered everywhere, swords were on display, and toys were scattered about. He crept into his bed and jumped under the sheets. After getting comfortable, Bort stared at the ceiling, unblinking. He couldn't sleep. Bort knew he had to go and see for himself if what Myco said was true. Besides, maybe Garlic would go with him. This gave Bort reassurance and peace of mind for the evening as his eyes grew heavy with exhaustion. With a giant yawn, he took the Dreamweaver train to pancake town.

TO BE CONTINUED

INTERLUDE 1

CHRONICLES OF THE REDWOODS:

Gaius Galin's Travels Among the Nine Realms

The morning rush of patrons that had piled in for breakfast now dwindled. Bort's restau-rant was almost empty, as many townsfolk chose to eat at first light to celebrate the holi-day. However, during dinner hours, like on the day of the Lifestream, would be overflowing with hungry patrons. Bort used the lull to refill his stocks and clean his kitchen.

Squeak, squeak, squeak…

Bort wiped down the dark wood countertop to a shine. Seeing his reflection, Bort smiled and nodded, satisfied with his work.

Ding, ding.

The bells tied to the corner of the entry door sounded, announcing a new arrival into the restaurant. Bort looked up to greet the customer and was met with two familiar faces. "Bo(Garlic! Xoey! Good Morning!)rt!" Bort said, happy to see his good friends again.

"Good morning, Bort!" the pair said in unison as they removed their shoes at the foyer and stepped up into the dining room. Bort smiled and gestured to a couple of empty stools at the bar where Garlic and Xoey sat down. Bort hopped off his stool and waddled over to grab a kettle of hot water and a new tin of tea. "Bo(The Philosopher's Soma Tea Shop in the Secret Hollow Grove District asked me to try their new blend of tea, Valiant Heart.)rt," Bort said and prepared three cups. "Bo(They would love for me to serve it, so tell me what you think.)rt." He poured the tea and made his way back to the counter and asked, "Bo(So what are your tummies rumbly for?)rt?"

"Full stack of mountain-berry pancakes smothered in riverberry syrup and a bowl of honey glazed fruit with honey drizzle," Xoey said, trying to contain her excitement.

Bort smiled, figuring she would ask for her usual dish, and turned to Garlic. "Bo(And, will it be berrydew pancakes drizzled in elderberry syrup, topped with strawberry whipped cream and a side of chokecherry jam?)rt?" He asked, figuring she'd choose her medicinal recipe.

Garlic chuckled and winked at Bort. "Please and thank you," she said in a smoky tone.

Bort nodded and hopped off his stool to prepare the breakfasts as the trio conversed.

TWENTY MINUTES LATER

Gulp, gulp, gulp.

"Ahh! Delicious!" Xoey exclaimed as she polished off her tea and banged the cup on the table. Her plate was laid bare, nearly clean enough to be put back in the cupboard. It wasn't like her, nor anyone, to gobble up her food as fast as Bort, but today she came in a distant second. She stood atop her stool with a very grave expression on her face and pointed at Bort, who stared up at her while cleaning his griddle. "You! We have important business to take care of," Xoey stated.

Bort continued to clean his griddle as he processed what Xoey said. His expression grew solemn. "Bort," he grunted and nodded his head. Bort scraped the griddle clean, wiped his flippers dirt-free, and removed his apron and hat. Xoey placed her fists on her sides as Bort darted around the counter and slid across the floor, not removing his gaze from Xo-ey's.

After a short pause, Bort procured Super Adventure Jump Hero 2: Curse of the Spooky Spiral Tower and held it overhead. Pleased, Xoey crossed her arms and nodded to the game con-sole. Bort turned his attention to it, puffed up his chest, and marched onward. He hit the power button of the vid screen, and it hummed to life, followed by the satisfying clunk of the game cartridge being inserted into the console. Bort reached for the power switch and paused, looking over his shoulder at Xoey. They both nodded at each other, prepared for what was to come. Turning back, Bort flipped the switch, and the game displayed on the screen.

Garlic, who had only just begun eating, watched the pair from the counter stomp off to the video game as if they were marching into battle. Not being a big gamer herself, she did not understand the weight of getting a new, exceedingly anticipated game to play for the first time, but she was keen enough to see that it was serious business to hardcore gamers. Especially if it could get Xoey to act so expressively. Garlic grabbed the wooden food tray and spun around to watch her two close friends play. Setting it on her lap, she neatly began eating, fixated on the vid screen.

A FEW MOMENTS LATER

"No! Go left! …Quick. Jump! Ah! Watch out," Xoey commanded, sitting beside Bort on the wooden floor of his restaurant in front of the screen.

Bort held the controller close to his body and leaned forward, his tongue sticking out, and focused on the first boss battle of Super Adventure Jump Hero II: Curse of the Spooky Spiral Tower. "Bo(Ha-ha! Got 'em!)rt!" Bort said devilishly as the character somersaulted over an attack and came crashing down with his spear.

The monster cried out and fell to the ground. "Yeah! You showed him!" Xoey said and nudged Bort with her shoulder. Bort turned his attention towards Xoey just as she gasped. "Huh! Bort," she said and pointed to the vid screen. "Second form!"

Bort looked at her, confused for a second, before realizing what she meant. He looked to the screen as the enemy bounded to his feet and began attacking Super Adventure Jump Hero. Bort flinched and fumbled the controller. As he regained his composure and pre-pared to fend off his assailant, the character was struck, fatally slain, and the screen faded to black. The words Game Over bled onto the dark background as an image of a grave-stone appeared. "Bo(What? No way!)rt!" Bort said, recognizing the higher difficulty in the game. Bort growled, hit the continue button, and gave it a few more tries, each time being struck down easily by the second form of the first boss.

"Hey... Hey! Pass it here! Let me try! I got an idea!" Xoey said. Bort passed her the con-troller, still seething from being dispatched with such ease. With a sour face and his arms now crossed, he watched on in anticipation, hoping Xoey could beat the monster.

Garlic's breakfast plate laid empty back on top of the counter. After spectating long enough, her eyes wandered around the restaurant admiring the decor. As she gazed behind the bar top on Bort's prep table, she saw one of her books poking out from under the counter where he stored his books of recipes and binders filled with the measurements she and Xoey helped him write with each new dish Bort created. She blinked and reached over to grab it from his book easel.

As she placed it in her lap, she looked up at Bort, who was immersed in the game alongside Xoey, and looked back down at the book, noticing different pieces of paper sticking out from the book displaying Bort's various notes and drawings to himself, many of them lit-tered with question marks and arrows pointed at different paragraphs.

Garlic's heart swelled as she figured he must be trying to read it as he waited through bak-ing times. She deduced the book must have been difficult for him on his own. Garlic looked back up at Bort, smiled, and cleared her throat. "Ahem... Hey, Bort?" she said in a sing-song voice.

Bort sat still before darting his gaze towards Garlic, who waived the book in front of her he had been working on. "While we're here, why don't we practice your reading?" Garlic said.

Bort stared with a deep-seated scowl. It was the last thing he wanted to do. "Gaius Galin's Travels Among the Nine Realms. Ya know, it's got a lot of really good stories in it."

Bort stared at the book. It had been a really hard one to try to read on his own, but he, to a great extent, wanted to know the stories it told. It was a book about the origins of many things, and about the many worlds and realms that evidently exist beyond Keevah. But Gai-us used a lot of big words that made it boring. Little by little, Bort's attention turned back to the game. Super Adventure Jump Hero was surrounding himself with light, before waving his hand and releasing an explosion of magic.

Noticing Bort's eyes flair at the spell cast in game, Garlic came up with an idea to get him to read with her. "Hey, Bort," Garlic said in a luscious voice as Bort shot a side glance at Garlic who continued waiving the book side to side. "You know... if you want to get bet-ter at magic, you will certainly need to improve your reading skills."

"Hah!" Xoey exclaimed, as she rained down a fire technique on the enemy. Bort's eyes shifted back to the screen; his furrowed brow now inverted as his mind was conflicted. Remembering the events of the morning, Bort wanted to put the work in to be better, and he so very badly wanted to cast spells like his friends. Not to mention, seeing Super Ad-venture Jump Hero on an epic adventure to save the world inspired Bort, but he also just wanted to plunge himself in the tale the video game wove.

A flicker of light came from where Garlic was seated that caught Bort's eye. His attention went back to her where she was still waiving the book in her hand, but in her free hand, conjured fire from the ether. His eyes grew wide. It was a cool magical flame spell! He real-ly wanted to be able to do that, too! But the game...

His eyes shifted back to the vid screen. Xoey, enthralled in the boss battle, was unaware of Garlic's attempts at influencing Bort. She used a lightning attack, which sent the hero blitz-ing into the creature. Once again, another flicker of light came from Garlic, which caught Bort's attention. Buzzes of electricity danced from her palm and into the atmosphere.

Bort huffed and resigned himself. "Bo(Beat him up real good, Xoey! I gotta do squiggle learning.)rt," Bort said, deflated. Xoey's eyes narrowed as she grunted and nodded, bol-stered by Bort's words. He got to his feet with an exasperat-ed face, and made his way to Garlic. Hopping up onto the stool next to her, he gripped the bottom of the seat and hop-slid next to her with his expression unwavering.

Garlic, pleased, set the book in her lap. "Don't worry. You'll get to play soon enough. And look! I got a chapter I think you'll really like," she said.

Still scowling, Bort stuck his head closer to the book with folded arms. "Now, I think you'll really like this one," Garlic said and flipped the pages to a chapter that showed a depiction of the majestic giant sequoias. Bort's expression changed to excitement, as he'd always been curious about the giant trees. Knowing this, Garlic continued, "You've always wanted to know about the giant sequoias, right? Well, according to Gaius Galin, these trees appar-ently are space-faring! He says they grow throughout the universe!"

Bort gasped, squeezed in closer to Garlic, and looked up into her eyes with childlike won-der. "Bo(Really?)rt?" he said.

Garlic shrugged and smiled. "Let's find out," she answered. Bort gazed down at the pages as Garlic began reading:

"In the great continent of Meliae, beyond the wandering thunderlands, is the vast Mukwa mountain range. Cradled throughout the mountains live two an-cient titans called the giant sequoias and the redwoods. For as long as time can remember, their origins have been largely unknown and spun within the myths and legends of Keevah. Like the many-limbed branches of these colossal sentinels, the stories of their geneses widely vary.

"However, I, Gaius Galin, have surmised a most clever hypothesis as to their be-ginnings. Through my ethereal journeys, it is my conjecture that somehow they travel the galaxy and sow themselves throughout the realms and worlds of this enigmatic universe. It is my belief that they traverse the stars, orphans to hopeful planets that will take them on as their own children.

"Outlandish some may say? Hah! I laugh at those who write me off as noth-ing more than a kooky old codger! Those poor fools have not seen what I've seen! Although, alas, I do admit, I cannot for certain speak to their precise origins. I have only seen them prevailing in a different dominion!

"Far, far beyond the reaches of what even our most sophisticated instru-ments and powerful mana can grasp lays a realm akin to Keevah. There inhabits only a single bipedal species, unlike the many found back home. Their average lifespan is rough-ly a hundred of their years. But in this strange land, the red-woods and giant se-quoias can be found!

"The trees are smaller in size, with redwoods reaching 379 feet up into the heav-ens, and the giant sequoias as wide as 31.4 feet. They are also much young-er, and their lifespan is only a fraction of the ones living in the Mukwa Mountain Range, between two and three thousand years. It is my assumption that there must be conditions on that planet that affect them in such ways. I suspect that one of the reasons why lifespans are so short is the extreme lack of mana that runs through that world. Yes, it must be a reason. I'm sure!

"But their similarities and looks are uncanny. The redwoods of this strange world create their own rain by capturing the fog on their branches, which contributes moisture to the forests during the dry season. They also provide habitats to many different animals and plants. Some of these lifeforms that inhabit these forests, the people of this planet, have dubbed them as something called 'endangered.' Black bears, wandering salamanders, pikas, roosevelt elk, rough-skinned newts, banana slugs, and their most primitive frogs, the tailed frogs, are but a few of the animals that call these forests home. And redwood sorrels, red snow plants, pitcher plants, and many mushrooms live alongside the giants. Like the redwoods back home, the ones here filter and shade the rivers and streams. They provide clean drinking wa-ter, and cool, clear water that fish like salmon require.

"Astonishingly, for as small as the trees are here, soil can still be found on the branches hundreds of feet from the ground. Like on Keevah, the soil comes from the large annual leaf shed, which collects at the base of the branches and decom-poses, leaving rich nutrients for life to thrive and for many plants and animals such as beetles, crickets, earthworms, millipedes, salamanders, fungi, ferns, and even young trees to live in. Even a forty-foot western hemlock has been spotted thriv-ing high within the canopies of these forests!

"The natives of this realm have even discovered that the mosses in the redwood canopy grow bacteria, called cyanobacteria, which takes nitrogen gas out of the atmosphere and converts it into nitrogen compounds that help plant life grow. It was originally believed that this natural fertilization in moss mats only happened on the forest floor. How wonderous! Even with the feeble pulses of mana, nature still seems to find a way. It seems the power of one's spirit must never be underesti-mated!

"Much the same as the trees in our realm do, they pull a significant amount of carbon dioxide from the atmosphere and store roughly five times more carbon aboveground than any other forest on their planet! Like the transporters we have, the inhabitants of this realm have very similar vehicles, with technology that even rivals our machines! Nevertheless, six fast-growing redwoods can sequester the same amount of carbon that is produced by driving one of their average 'cars' for a full year! I wonder how much carbon the redwoods and giant sequoias can seize in our world? An experiment for another day!"

Garlic finished and was ready to continue onto the next page. Somewhere amid her reading, Bort had snuck onto her lap and was studying the many intricate drawings and findings of Gaius Galin. He snapped his head up to Garlic. "Bo(Wowie! Do you think all of this is true?)rt?" Bort said with enthusiasm.

Garlic smiled and shrugged. "I don't think any of us really know. He makes a good point though. Besides, all of this was written long, long ago. It could be just stories of an ancient oddball wizard. His claims are as remarkable now as they were then," she said. Bort brought his head down and studied the illustrations once more. "But, everything he has said about the redwoods and giant sequoias are true," Garlic added.

Bort snapped his head back up at her with surprise and excitement in his eyes. "Bo(Really?)rt?" Bort said and looked around his restaurant, which was nestled inside an old giant sequoia. "Bo(In the giant sequoias, here is home to a Bort.)rt," Bort said as he turned the page for Garlic.

Bort gasped at what he saw: images of these magnificent trees on fire, cut down, and their habitats nearly all but destroyed.

Garlic was prepared for this, yet the look in Bort's eyes still caught her off guard. She closed her eyes and nodded as they continued reading.

"With their behaviors thoroughly examined, one cannot deny that the redwoods and giant sequoias of Keevah are identical! Only in lifespan, size, and mana do they vary. Alas, I record this with a very heavy heart, unlike the many Keevahlings who coexist with their natural world, the peoples of this world, to put it bluntly, do not. Here, in their twenty-first century, a fraction of their redwood forests remain. Before their year of 1850 AD, roughly two million acres of redwood habitat sprawled through their world. Today, five percent of that has survived. Of that five percent, twenty-three percent is protected. In these forests, black bears and the Humboldt marten were commonplace. Now, ninety-five percent of these creatures have vanished.

"The reasons for their destruction are plenty but can be traced back to the mid-1800s during a strange event they call the Gold Rush, where many flocked to a place they called California, which was much like a kingdom within a kingdom. Like on Keevah, gold holds significant value there, yet there, they go to many lengths to obtain this precious metal. This Gold Rush created a stifling demand for lumber. Thus, the ancient old-growth redwoods and giant sequoias suffered from unbridled logging. They were harvested, valued for their strength, resilience, and, of course, their beauty. This was further bolstered by a dreadful earthquake in 1906, which decimated a town they called San Francisco.

"Even to this day, they are still facing many threats. Here, their social structure and economy have fed a corporate machine that is never appeased and hungers forevermore, thus fostering devious methods to continue its never-ending urge to consume. Where there is a will, there is a way, I presume, even if it is less than honorable. One of these methods is using the habitat of the redwoods to farm an herb called marijuana. It is used medicinally, recreationally, and can be used to make a plethora of different materials! A handy herb, indeed! Though many who farm this crop use water-diverting methods, which cut valuable sources of water from these forests, and they use volatile pesticides and rodenticides that can poison the planet and spread toxins throughout the forest. Since the rodenticides do not kill immediately, the animals that consume this noxious substance are then eaten by owls, fish, black bears, etcetera. And, like the animals who initially consumed this toxin, it is then spread to them. These animals then suffer a very painful and agonizingly ghastly death.

"Another vicious method that is used for personal gain is burl poaching. Redwood burls are large natural protrusions prized for their intricately patterned wood that can weigh hundreds of pounds and can earn these poachers a great bounty. The burls are most prolific on the oldest trees, and being full of stem cells, they play a critical role in the trees' regeneration. Removing these burls exposes vulnerable heartwood to further damage, may deny the tree its primary means of reproduction, and can result in the felling of redwood trees to access burls higher up on the trunks.

"Astonishingly, the destruction of redwood habitats is also due to more "proper" means such as the land being converted to real estate properties and vineyards. It eludes me how and why they choose to destroy the beauty of their world, which takes eons to produce, for houses and fruit…"

The words on the page came to an end, and the two paused. "Bo(Wh… Why?)rt?" was all Bort could say as he looked back up at Garlic. She shook her head and shrugged. "You know, Bort, even our own history is filled with things we would rather not remember we did. Sometimes, it comes from simply not knowing, or greed, and even old systems of be-liefs," she said.

Bort looked back down at the book. "Bo(I understand that sometimes we need to use trees to live in, or we need to use things so we can do cool things, but it is important to take care of the things we take.)rt," he said. "Bo(I think I wanna go plant some more trees, to make sure I thank this old tree I live in.)rt."

Garlic smiled. "I think that is a great idea, Bort," she said. "We are lucky here in Lemnear. I think Lemnearians have a very similar mindset when it comes to such ideas. In fact, it is one big reason why Lemnear was founded — striving to help the individual, like with your pan-cake shop."

Bort looked away from Garlic's gaze and at the old tree he lived in. "Bo(A lot of people came here to help me.)rt," he said and looked around at everything in his restaurant. "Bo(My pots and pans, these chairs, the video games, the ingredients… All were painstak-ingly made.)rt," Bort said.

His little brain worked and he smiled. "Bo(And with all their hard work to help me, I will help them to make sure they have yummy food to eat, always! And that they always leave happy! I will make sure they eat healthy food and can recover here so that we can keep helping each other!)rt!" Bort said.

"All for one, and one for all," Garlic commented.

Bort sat up straighter, and a little prouder. "Bo(Yeah! If I want what's best for you, and you want what is best for me, then we can all do super-cool things!)rt!"

Garlic pet Bort's head and moved her hand to turn the page.

"Bo(No, wait!)rt!" Bort said and slapped his flippers on the book, preventing her from moving onto the next page.

Garlic pulled back. "What's wrong?" she said, concerned.

With a solemn face, Bort looked up into Garlic's eyes, filled with burning conviction. "Bo(Lemme study the images a bit longer. That way, I can really re-member what can hap-pen when we are not careful. I need to make sure I never, ever forget.)rt," Bort said. He took a deep breath, covered his ears, and pressed his face to the pages, doing his best to take in every little detail and make it an important remembory.

After nearly turning blue, Bort puffed out his breath and dropped his flippers to his sides. "Bo(Okay… I'm ready.)rt," he said between breaths and turned the page.

"Is it that difficult to coexist and see the many gifts the trees can offer? Even with their own research, it has been proven that being in nature balances health and wellbeing! Just viewing scenes of nature reduces feelings of anger, fear, and stress, only to induce more pleasant feelings. It can even reduce more physical symptoms such as high blood pressure and heart rate, muscle tension, mortality, and the production of stress hormones in the body! Studies have even shown that people undergoing medical procedures that are either in, or simply viewing nature, have more pain tolerance, appeared to have fewer negative side effects, and spend less time in the hospital.

"There in that world, the people have an addiction to vid screens. Although they are a useful tool and can connect people all around their world instanta-neously, in many ways, this has served to further divide and isolate them. This has exponen-tially caused the rate of depression to soar, a loss of empathy and altruism, and heightened the risk of death! When surrounded by nature, individ-uals have re-ported knowing more people, having stronger senses of unity with neighbors, and having a deeper feeling of belonging. This in turn builds a greater sense of commu-nity, reduces crime, lowers levels of aggression and violence between domestic partners, and makes people better able to cope with life's demands and the stresses of living in poverty.

"How dreadful! I can only deduce that a major role in the destruction of these magnificent titans is the inhabitants of that realm! I hope that my research into un-locking the enigma of the redwoods is not cut short by the recklessness of these lifeforms. It is my hopes that upon my next return to this place, the peo-ple would have come to their senses, and done something to aid in the recovery of the red-woods. There are plenty of natives there that understand this and do what they can in order to protect their world from themselves.

"I postulate that the inhabitants of that realm cannot simply rely on donating to groups or by "liking" posts on social media constructs. Donating to organiza-tions are very helpful, but their world is riddled with people who always say what they do not mean, and always do what they do not say. It is a realm wrought with con-fusing information that is used to manipulate and sustain a person's or or-ganiza-tion's financial gain and influence. It requires an individual's due diligence to be as sure as can be that their chosen organization upholds their word and utilizes their funding for what they claim to be about.

"On the flipside, there are many who think they are part of change by saying words on a social media construct that has nothing more to do with anything be-yond a fleeting false sensation of instant gratification, a way to pat themselves on the back and say, 'I am helping.' I believe that even if the individual feels powerless to help, there is much they can do. Remember, everything began with an idea. Learn about the redwoods and spread the information about them, find honest organizations to be part of or donate to, write to those voted into power to ad-vocate for you, and, probably the most important of all, do not fund corpo-rations, banks, or products that are involved in the destruction of the redwood habitats in any way.

"I surmise, some of the most crucial components are knowledge, the indi-vidual, and the community. Learning about your ephemeral world and the fragile ecosys-tems within it, as well as the constructed systems people have put in place that ef-fect these ecologies may give birth to new ideas, different approaches, and valua-ble insight to not only destroy the comforts of living but coexist with the natural world. It is up to the individual to make the step and begin an arduous task. You may be constrained by economic situations, or reside in different re-gions and the like, but you can still begin gardens and grow with what is available to you. Re-member, everything that is, once began with only an idea. Lastly is the community. Together we are stronger. Sometimes the voices of the individual fall upon deaf ears. When bolstered by a community, that whisper turns into a shout. The many individuals that make up the community can offer unique skills, talents, and ideas. Even if the lackeys of the kingdom decide to destroy the redwood habi-tats, they will have no choice but to bow to the people that choose not to follow."

The pictures on these pages depicted both possible outcomes, and Bort reviewed them thoroughly. "Bo(I sure hope they did something to turn things around and made this one come true,)rt," he said and pointed to the illustrations of the proliferation of the red-woods.

"I hope they did, as well," Garlic said.

Bort looked up at Xoey playing Super Adventure Jump Hero 2. "Bo(You know, I really love video games. But I love the nature I am lucky enough to live in, as well.)rt," Bort said.

"Yes, there is nothing wrong with being able to enjoy those things, Bort. But it is important to take care of the world around you, and your health. Being active and enjoying nature is vital to a fulfilling life, because without it, there wouldn't even be a thought of a video game," Garlic said.

Bort studied the pages. "Bo(You know, I bet it is probably scary to step out of line and go with your gut. But I think it is important to make your own way for yourself. I think, there will always be something to stand in your way, even if it is your own self. But we can't ex-pect everything to be done for us or go our way.) rt," Bort began as he dug deeply to pro-cess how Gaius Galin's story made him feel and what the events at the lake had taught him. "Bo(It is not about having other people be responsible for what I think is right. I can only be responsible for what I choose to do and accept the outcomes of how I may be treated. Even if it means people make fun of me. I can only lead by the example I set, and if I want to see something change, I need to first change that in myself.)rt."

Garlic drew back, speechless. Bort's words were very profound, and they made a lot of sense. "Wow, Bort. Yeah, I think so, too," she mustered to say.

Bort hummed and nodded. He paused a second before saying, "Bo(You know what? If this story is true, and if I could somehow go back in time and be with the people who chose to help the giant sequoias, I would tell them that no matter how alone they might feel, or how hard the task may seem, their example by action attracted another to do the same. And I would be there with seed and shovel in flipper, if I had to do it single-flipperly.)rt," Bort said, and stared down at his flippers, that he then balled into fists.

Garlic smiled and nodded, petting Bort once more, acknowledging Bort without words. Bort looked up at Garlic. "Bo(Thank you for reading it to me and helping me learn and understand.)rt," Bort said.

"And thank you for the wonderful breakfast that will give me health and energy to work through the day," Garlic replied.

Bort closed the book and jumped off Garlic's lap. "Bo(Let's go plant a tree!) rt!" Bort said.

Garlic smiled and got to her feet and stretched. "That sounds like a great idea," she said.

Xoey stomped over to Bort and Garlic with stiff shoulders and narrow eyes. "Here," was all Xoey said as she handed Bort the controller.

Bort looked at her and at the video game. The same bloody Game Over scrawled down the screen. "Bo(Wanna come help us plant a tree, Xoey?)rt?" Bort asked.

"Yeah," Xoey answered, still angered.

ONE HOUR LATER

"Ahh! Well, that was satisfying!" Xoey said, her spirits lifted and her mood vastly improved.

"I'd say so," Garlic said, enjoying the cool forest breeze.

Bort looked up at his two friends as he shoveled soil around the tiny seedling. "Bo(One day this tree will be ginormous! I'm gonna call it Pizza!)rt!" Bort said.

"Let's each take turns caring for Pizza," Garlic said as the trio smiled and nodded at one another. "Okay, it's getting late. How about we meet up sometime later?" she added as the three turned around and headed around Bort's house.

"Bo(Yeah, I got super-not-so-secret secret adventure-hero training to do.)rt," Bort said.

"Sounds like a plan. Why don't we meet up for Realms and Ravens night? We could eat out and then head to Level Up to get us a strategy guide for Super Jump Hero," Xoey suggest-ed.

"Oh, that sounds fun," Garlic said.

All the while, Bort was nodding vigorously, excited for the planning as they made their way down the cobblestone path.

"Redwood Forest Facts." Save the Redwoods League, 27 Oct. 2017, www.savethered-woods.org/redwoods/interactive-redwood-forest-facts/.
"How Does Nature Impact Our Wellbeing?" Taking Charge of Your Health & Wellbeing, www.takingcharge.csh.umn.edu/how-does-nature-impact-our-wellbeing.

INTERLUDE 2

The Big Book of Remem-beries #478:

Tell Me an Amazing Story!

Bort stared at his reflection in the bathroom mirror, brushing his teeth and flossing his tusks as the day's events echoed in his mind. It still felt so unbelievable. Bort took a sip of water, swished it around, gargled, and spit it into the sink. His gaze was fixated on his eyes, peering past them and into his thoughts as he washed his flippers and his face. The cold water certainly reminded him that today was no dream. With the squeak of the knob, the water shut off, and he dried his face and made his way to his bedroom.

With the evening wash-up done, Bort's next task was one of his favorites. He knelt beside his bed and pulled open one of the drawers. Besides cool-looking rocks, shells, marbles, capsule toys, and insta-capsules was a series of notebooks adorned with Bort's drawings, stickers, and warnings. On them, Bort had scrawled, Big Book of Remembories, and they were numbered by volume. Bort smiled, pulled out the top book, and thumbed to a blank page. He set the open book carefully beside him and, from his end table, got a pack of crayons, markers, and a pencil.

Making sure to catalog his days, especially memories, Bort held this ritual to his evenings in high regard. Bort, terrified of his amnesia, wanted to make sure he would never lose his memories again. He went through his room, setting up his figurines, stuffed toys, and his plants in a way so they had their eyes on him as he plopped himself in the middle of the rug in his room. It was easier for Bort to tell a story of his day, rather than draw and write it in complete silence. Looking around at his audience, Bort's smile grew.

"Bo(Good evening, everybody.)rt," Bort said and then muffled his mouth with his flippers. "Bo(Good evening, Bort.)rt," he said in a higher-pitched voice, pretending to be his audi-ence.

"Bo(By the pancakes guys! I have the most unbelievable rememborries to share with you all.)rt," Bort said. "Bo(Really? Tell us. Tell us.)rt," he said in a lower voice this time.

"Bo(Today, I woke up, went down the Gun-Tekk slide, and then worked on Hot Dog, which sank… But then Doughnut helped me think of things that were good! And then, I did su-per-not-so-secret secret-hero training! But Mr. Fluffy Feets won… I looked at the misty Bronwyn Falls, then I made more yummy food! But then, I was feeling yuckie and went for a walk by myself and met a giant! Her name was Zankiras. I asked her to help with Hot Dog, but she couldn't. I hope she comes over to eat, and I hope I can do something so she can help me. Then I wandered the market and almost got blown away by a strong wind as a shop I never saw before showed up! The name of the store is too hard for me to remem-ber. But I met Thoth, who owns it! He gave me a magic book that likes my guts or some-thing. It's called The Enchiridion! This helped me feel not yucky any-more and makes me wanna cook more! But Myco came for dinner and said there was a monster.)rt," he said all at once, and showed his audience the Enchiridion.

Bort looked around at his audience and nodded before picking up some markers and began drawing the day's events in his book of remembories.

Squeak, squeak, squeak…

The sound of the marker against the paper filled the silence. Bort looked back up at his audience, who stared at him with unfettered attention. He paused for a while. This wasn't the first time he had felt as if they were staring at him waiting for more. It even made him feel uncomfortable. Bort's brain worked to find a solution. Hmm, maybe the telling of my day is too short, he thought just as he was hit with inspiration.

"Bo(Hey! I know, guys! Why don't I tell you my remembories like a story from now on?)rt?" he said as his eyes grew in excitement at his own words. "Bo(Yeah! Yeah! What a great idea! Tell us in a story!)rt!" Bort said, muffling his voice in a high pitch.

"Bo(Wowie! Okay! If you say so!)rt!" Bort said and threw his arms up in the air. He was thrilled at the idea of having his day be told like a story. Just like the books he had read or the video games he had played, he would now have his days told. Bort shook with anticipa-tion, trying to keep his composure.

"Bo(Okay, here goes nothing!)rt!" Bort exclaimed. "Bo(Today, when I woke up… erm…)rt…" he stuttered. It already sounded weird to him. He stared up at his forehead and played with his tusks as he looked for a way to tell his story. Think-ing back to the tales he had read, they never really said "I".

Bort turned away from his audience, scratched his chin, and mumbled to himself. Just then, it clicked in his head. "Bo(Oh! I know!)rt!" Bort said. He cleared his throat and took a big deep breath. "Bo(Bort woke up after watch-ing the Lifestream with his friends.)rt," Bort began, telling his day in the third person. However, something peculiar happened, Bort be-gan thinking how to better detail his story. It wouldn't do just to explained what had hap-pened. In all the stories he had enjoyed, they would explain how the character felt, what they thought, or why they did what they did. So Bort started doing the same. "Bo(Watching the Lifestream with his friends really made Bort feel loved and closer to those he cared deeply about.)rt," he continued.

Bort's eyes widened. He knew he loved his dear friends, but to put it that way, he realized how much he had taken them for granted because he saw them daily. "Bo(Bort felt like he never wanted to miss another event if it could not be shared with those he cared about. Without the people in his life, those things could seem pretty boring, Bort thought.)rt," he said.

Bort took a moment and looked down at his Big Book of Rememborics. This was really im-portant to him, and he had to write it down!

Squeak, squeak, squeak…

Bort made a little drawing of himself hugging Garlic and Xoey as they sat un-derneath the colorful night sky, with small explanations of what they were doing. Bort nodded and con-tinued his story. "Bo(After they left, Bort was left alone with all of his thinkies that made him feel a little yucky. Bort knew that everything felt good, but he knew deep down that he needed to do more to make sure he could make his dreams come true…)rt…" Bort trailed off. His eyes grew a bit somber as he recalled the feelings of that night alone.

He shook his head and drew in his book, making sure to detail everything he was feeling and how the day went. Bort wanted to make sure he could learn from these new insights, so he could eventually make the necessary changes, so he wouldn't feel those bad feelings anymore.

Bort took a moment to think. This little exercise he was doing sure showed him a lot about himself. Standing back from his day and viewing it in the third person gave great in-sight to his feelings and how he processed his emotions.

"Bo(Wowie, guys! I gotta make sure to tell every rembory like this!)rt!" Bort said to his audience in excitement. Bort finished his drawing and explana-tions before continuing his storytelling, going back to write down every new insight that came with each event he'd experienced in the day.

Rivas, A. (2014, June 10). Writing in third person helps stressed people understand their circum-stances more wisely. Medical Daily. https://www.medicaldaily.com/writing-third-person-helps-stressed-people-understand-their-circumstances-more-wisely-287460.